# Shadow Wars: LitRPG Adventure Fantasy

**LitRPG: Shadow For Hire, Volume 3**

Adam Drake

Published by Adam Drake, 2018.

This is a work of fiction. Similarities to real people, places, or events are entirely coincidental.

SHADOW WARS: LITRPG ADVENTURE FANTASY

**First edition. August 21, 2018.**

Copyright © 2018 Adam Drake.

ISBN: 979-8201482442

Written by Adam Drake.

Shadow Wars
(Shadow For Hire Series)
by
Adam Drake
Copyright 2018 © Adam Drake

# Shadow Wars

**I'm a loot-hunting adventurer, not a general.**

I play online MMOs for exciting quests, to level my character and find cool loot. Not to lead armies.

But now I have to fight a battle to get the quest item I desperately need.

I've never commanded troops or built bases or strategized an attack more complex than a dungeon raid. When it comes to war, I'm a complete noob.

Yet, defeat isn't an option. I've got to win or everything I've worked so hard for will be lost.

So, they want a war?

I'll give them one.

# CHAPTER ONE

My view-screen suddenly went dark, and a message appeared before me:

*You Have Died.*

Still shaking with the adrenaline rush of combat, I stared at the floating text in shock. What the heck? How did that happen?

I'd been engaged in a ferocious knockdown, drag-out fight with an Elite Cyclops who happened to be the final obstacle in completing my quest. For two full weeks, I followed an elaborate chain of interlinked quests all leading to a final goal: The Lost War Banner of Y'Godda.

After a lot of quest related angst and bother, the location of the War Banner had finally been revealed to me; a magically sealed cave hidden in the Forest of Dreams. The elation of my discovery soon evaporated when I arrived at the cave to find the Elite Cyclops guarding it, massive obsidian club in hand.

Assessing the monster gave me pause. He was more powerful than me but not by much. Still, given everything I'd been through, giving up wasn't an option. We fought for nearly an hour. He, with is club and innate Cyclops abilities (like the One Eyed Death Stare), and me with sword and bow.

My Shadow class granted me Shadow Form, the ability to effectively turn almost invisible. When he swung at me, I'd activate my Shadow Form and dodge away, only to reappear and strike at him from a different angle.

It was going great for a while, too. Despite the Cyclops' near infinite reservoir of hit points, I'd chipped away at his health until it dropped to roughly fifteen percent remaining. Then disaster struck – I got cocky. Which, it turns out, is a fatal mistake when dealing with an Elite monster.

I'd fired a Disorientation arrow that temporarily blinded him. But, apparently, the Cyclops race has a strong resistance to blinding attacks – go figure. When I switched to my sword and ran in close for a final kill-strike, the Cyclops had recovered. The towering humanoid dropped his club and, before I could even react, clapped his meaty hands together.

The result of using the Thunder Clap ability sent out a concussive wave which threw my little avatar pinwheeling across the clearing to splat against a tree.

My view-screen distorted to simulate being nearly knocked out and disoriented. When my vision cleared, I found the Cyclops towering over me and massive obsidian club descending fast.

I tried to roll out of the way, but not fast enough.

Now I stared at a death screen. Something I hadn't experienced in what felt like ages.

With no more fight to engage in, I masochistically scrolled through the combat log at the bottom left of my view-screen. Here was a detailed statistical account of the fight. Just from these messages alone, things had looked good for me.

*Vivian Valesh strikes Elite Cyclops in the left leg for 220 hit points of damage.*

*Vivian Valesh hits Elite Cyclops with an arrow in the right shoulder for 125 hit points of damage.*

And on, and on it read with similar messages, all showing how I'd bled away the creature's hit points to almost nothing.

But then there was the final message.

*Elite Cyclops crits Vivian Valesh with Obsidian Club of Smashing. Elite Cyclops critical damage bonus is x5. Vivian Valesh takes 3,500 hit points of damage.*

*Vivian Valesh is dead.*

3,500 hit points of damage. Yup, that killed me alright, considering I was down to 700 hit points at that point.

I sighed and sagged back in my simulation suit its rigging and attachments pulling at my body. Normally my view was of the game's world and moving about in the suit went unnoticed. But confronted by the blackness of character death, its apparatus felt more prominent.

Now what? I thought, trying not to sulk. I could go back to work, but the IceStation was humming along just fine without me loitering about. My job was effectively to simply be present as the station AI performed all the necessary tasks to harvest ice on Callisto. Instead of twiddling my thumbs I play Unlimited Fantasy Worlds Online. Corny title, freaking amazing game!

But now my character was dead.

Death meant I had to start all over again. Never mind the time wasted trying to locate the Lost War Banner of Y'Godda. All the progress my character made attaining levels over the months had been wiped out in one fell swoop of a crit-charged obsidian club.

Such is the fickle nature of playing the game.

Restarting my character meant suffering time in one of the dreaded newbie zones, areas filled with simple quests designed to coddle new characters through their first few levels.

I silently cursed myself for being overconfident. The image of the club filled my vision.

My frustration had gotten the better of me. I even considered slipping out of my simulation suit and just walking away from the game. (Sacrilege!)

But I was an addict. Even in death, I needed my fix.

I gave the view-screen my full attention. Sensing my eye movement the game faded the death message away in preparation for bringing up the character creation screen.

But it didn't.

Blackness, like a void, stared back at me.

I wiggled my fingers and made gestures with my hands. Nothing happened. Did the game get hung up? Although an incredibly rare event, the game did bug-out on occasion, sending players back to their login screens.

But no login screen appeared.

After a few moments of finger karate and arm flapping, I decided to make an angry call to Customer Support. But before I did, a new message appeared before me.

*Amara Frostwalker has used a Ruby of Resurrection on you.*

*Do you wish to be resurrected? Yes/No?*

Stunned, it was all I could do but stare at the screen. A resurrection. What are the odds? Me, way out in the middle of nowhere all on my own and someone walks by and offers to save me.

Amara Frostwalker? Didn't know this person as far as I could remember. But I'll remember now.

I selected Yes.

The blackness of my view-screen dissolved away.

Blue sky filled my vision, and I realized my avatar was laying on the ground. An elven woman's face peered down at me.

"Hello," said the elf. "You should be okay now."

I sat up, blinking in amazement.

"Wow," I said and jumped to my feet. "Now this is a first."

"A first what?" asked the elf. "First time dying, or first time getting killed by a Cyclops?"

"First time being resurrected," I said with a smile. Then I looked about in alarm. "The Cyclops?"

The elven woman pointed to the edge of the clearing. A large body was splayed out on the grass. Its huge eye stared sightlessly into the sky.

"How did you kill him?" I asked while checking the icons on my view-screen. Health was at maximum and no indications of any lingering effects.

The elf shrugged. "While he was smashing your head with the club, over and over, I snuck up and back-stabbed him. Took him out in one go." She smiled impishly. "It was easy because you'd taken his health down so low."

"Yeah," I said. "Thanks for that. And for resurrecting me. It was such a surprise. I'm not use to the kindness of passing strangers. Most players are pretty hardcore." That was an understatement. Considering how high the stakes were in this game, you had to be really motivated to save another player. Especially when it might mean you could die, too. Instead of one person being sent to the newbie zone, it could easily become two.

The elf woman nodded and looked a little nervous. She said, "I'm Amara Frostwalker, by the way. But you'd already know that now from the system message."

I let out a nervous laugh. "I'm Vivian Valesh, pleased to meet you. And I really mean that." I laughed a little more and as we shook hands, I got a better look at her.

Like me, she was a Shadow class character, only her race was elven. She wore a nearly identical outfit as mine; hooded cloak, leather leggings and vest. But unlike my solid black garb, hers was a muted gray, with different tones.

Across her back was a quiver full of arrows. On her thigh was a sheathed short sword. She stood a head shorter than me with a narrow frame which was typical elven bone structure.

Her eyes were a bright emerald green, with hair a snowy white pulled back under her hood.

"No worries," Amara said. "It's not every day I get to rescue a legend."

"Legend? Me?" I said, taken aback.

Amara's expression changed to one of disbelief. "Yeah! You're Vivian Valesh, the Shadow who defeated the Demon King and got the Legendary Cloak of Shadows."

"Oh, right," I said. "That." Uh-oh, I thought. Did I have a groupie on my hands?

Amara beamed. "And you killed *the* Ogden Trite! The richest and most powerful player in the entire game."

"I'd argue against him being the richest and most powerful. But I'm sure he thinks that. And still does." I am not a Player Killer by heart, but Ogden Trite had put me in a position where I had to take action. Lucky for me, it worked out in my favor.

Amara nodded with enthusiasm. "Your exploits are all over the net. Engraved forever in the wikis, too."

Not sure what was expected of me I decided to make her an offer. "Let me pay you back for the Ruby of Resurrection. It's the least I can do."

Amara shook her head. "No, not at all. I didn't buy it. It was a random drop on a Daily Quest awhile back. Just never had the need to use it until now. I'm a solo player, mostly."

"Cool," I said. Well, that would save me a huge pile of gold I couldn't really afford.

Amara suddenly said, "I've gotta run, so I'll leave you to your quest." She turned to walk out of the clearing and into the forest.

Before she left I asked, "Hey, can I ask you a question?"

Amara paused at the tree line. "Sure."

"Why'd you do it? Why'd you save me?"

The elven woman raised an eyebrow in thought. Then said, "Because you never know when helping someone else might pay off in the future." And with that, she vanished into the trees.

Huh, I thought. Okay, sounds reasonable. Kinda. But a little strange. What she had done was big, yet she wanting nothing in return.

I shrugged and gave my character stats a quick once over.

*Name: Vivian Valesh*
*Race: Human*
*Class: Thief*
*Subclass: Shadow*
*Level: 45, 18% toward next level*

*Hit Points: 1250, Mana: 120*
*Attributes:*
*Strength: 34*
*Agility: 46*
*Constitution: 40*
*Wisdom: 15*
*Intelligence: 15*
*Charisma: 20*
*Main Skills: (Level 3 or greater)*
*Archery: Level 8, 81%*
*Acrobatics: Level 3, 55%*
*Climbing: Level 7, 20%*
*Dodge: Level 7, 12%*
*Parry: Level 6, 20%*
*Sneak: Level 7, 42%*
*Swords: Level 9, 72%*
*Minor Skills: (Under level 3 - Select to view)*

Having been stuck at level 44 for what seemed like forever, I'd hit 45 a couple of days prior. I'd stuffed two Attribute points into Constitution, bumping up my hit points, and one point into Strength.

My 3 Ability points went into a brand new ability I'd wanted for a long time.

*Multi-Shot Ability (3/6)*

*+15% Damage, -30 second to cooldown.*

*Allows for four normal arrows to be shot at the same time. Cannot be used with special arrows. 2 minutes 30 seconds cooldown. Next level grants +20% Damage bonus and -40 seconds to cooldown.*

Nice, huh? I originally was only going to put two points into it, but the third point gave four arrows to shoot at once, instead of three. Couldn't resist.

Satisfied everything was fine, I swiped away the stats and turned to look at a large stone door set within a nearby outcrop of rocks. The door's surface was covered with a magical barrier which rippled like a rainbow as sunlight played across it.

My elation at being brought back to life morphed into an equally thrilling feeling: accomplishment.

This was the end of my long quest chain, the final stop. Had the stupid Cyclops not nuked me, I could claim to have finished it all on my own. But who was I to argue with luck? I stepped around the corpse of the Cyclops and stood before the sealed door.

With an outstretched arm, I placed a hand against the barrier. Having completed all the steps necessary to get here, I was now allowed to pass. The barrier dissolved at my touch. Gears *thunked* and turned from within. The stone door then slowly opened, sliding to one side and disappearing into the rock itself. A dark passage presented itself.

Finally, I thought. If nearly being sent to the newbie zone was the cost of getting here, then so be it. Totally worth it.

I crossed the threshold, then stopped. Something wasn't right.

I spun around to look back outside at the clearing. Grass and trees swayed with a breeze.

For long moments, I waited and watched. Nothing changed. Eventually, the corpse of cyclops faded away, the game's way of cleaning house. Bodies of opponents and monsters did not rot as they might in the real world. Of that I was grateful. I'd be responsible for a lot of dead bodies cluttering the ground across the gaming universe. Thousands of them. Tens of thousands, even.

I shook my head. There was nothing. I was just on edge after having my head crushed.

I followed the passage deeper.

It opened up to a large cavern, and I paused, stunned.

The entire floor was covered in skeletons, more than could be counted. Some were clad in armor while others clasped swords. They formed a macabre carpet of death. And each one held out an arm and pointed with a skeletal hand to the center of the cavern.

There, upon a rocky rise, stood a banner flag which billowed from an undetectable breeze. A shaft of sunlight fell from a hole in the ceiling to envelope the banner, causing it to emanate with a magical glow.

The Lost War Banner of Y'Godda.

"Sweet," I said, impressed with the ambiance. Talk about a cool room to hold the final quest item. Gotta love it when the developers go the extra mile to make the game feel even more special than it already was.

A row of skulls formed a pathway through the skeletons from where I stood to the banner. With a quick look around I cautiously walked across it, wary of a trap.

I crossed and soon stood before the banner. Nothing happened. No traps, no worries. Time to cross off another quest from my quest log.

I sheathed my sword, grabbed the banner's wooden pole with both hands and pulled.

Nothing happened.

Frowning, I pulled again. The banner didn't budge. Not an inch.

What the heck?

I looked down to see someone else was also grabbing onto the banner's wooden pole with two hands.

I gasped in surprise. It was Amara

She'd dropped out of Shadow form and grabbed the banner the same moment I did.

"What the heck?" I blurted. Why was she here, and what did she want with the banner?

Amara's face contorted with anger. "This is mine, FILTERED. Let go of it!" My language filter kept me from hearing the colorful and nasty words some people threw at me.

Amara tried to pull the banner away, but it held fast, stuck in the rocks.

"This is not yours," I said, confused. I tried to pull the banner away from her, but it still didn't budge.

For a few moments we both feebly tugged at the banner but it didn't yield to either of us.

Frustrated with this nonsense I decided to unsheathe my sword, but was struck with a thought.

What would happen to the banner when I let it go? Technically, it was the final item to obtain in my quest chain, but could it still be claimed by Amara? She'd grabbed it the exact moment I did, and as a result the game hadn't assigned the item to either one of us, yet.

"What the heck do you think you're doing?" I said, anger flaring in my chest. "This is my quest item. I earned it."

Amara, still holding steadfast to the banner, tried to kick at me with her closest leg. I blocked it with a knee.

"Open world quest, FILTERED," she said, almost spitting out the words. "Why should I spend weeks trying to finish a stupid quest chain when I could just wait for an idiot like you to finish it for me?"

She kicked again, and I blocked it.

Unfortunately, she was right. This quest was open to anyone, and so its quest items were available to any other player. They didn't need to follow the entire quest to get the reward, they just needed the items.

This was an item based quest. I needed the Lost Banner to take to the final quest giver to get the reward. But Amara hadn't bothered to do the quest herself, she wanted to steal the final item and claim the quest reward for herself, without doing any of the work.

Then it hit me.

"You resurrected me so I'd open the sealed door!" I said, almost shouting.

Amara laughed, like a witch's cackle. "You dumb FILTERED. Now you figured it out. Well done, FILTERED."

She certainly had a potty mouth, and the more we kicked at each other and tried to wrestle the banner free, the more likely I was going to start swearing, too.

For several moments we kicked at one another, and Amara would punctuate each one with a filtered curse.

This was ridiculous. The moment either one of us let go of the banner, the game would assign it to the other.

What could I do? Wait until one of us had kicked the other to death?

Turned out I didn't have to come up with a solution. As chance would have it, the solution presented itself.

The cavern suddenly brightened, and a large figure materialized next to us.

Both Amara and I paused in our kickfest to look in amazement at the new arrival.

A dwarf stood next to the banner, frowning at us. He was clad in heavy white armor. A voluminous red beard hung down to his waist where twin hand axes were tucked into his belt.

Although surprised at his appearance, it was the name above his head which caused me to gasp in surprise.

Y'Godda the Warrior King (Spirit)

"Oh, FILTERED," said Amara.

Y'Godda's frown deepened. "What do we have here?" he said, his baritone voice echoing around the chamber. "Two adventurers are trying to claim my banner? Yet, only one may have such an honor."

He looked between us. "Who shall it be?"

Not realizing the spirit was asking rhetorically, Amara blurted out an answer. "Me! It's me that should have it! The honor should be mine!"

Y'Godda turned to fix his ghostly eyes on me.

Figuring he wanted an answer, I said, "I have been seeking your banner for a long time, sire. The quest has been difficult and fraught with peril. It was by my hand that the magical seal on the door to this place opened. Only the rightful quester could do that." I swallowed hard when he didn't immediately respond. "The banner is mine by right." I finished.

Y'Godda's eyes bounced between the two of us in contemplation.

Come on! I wanted to shout. This is my quest, so this is my quest item!

I scowled at Amara who sneered at me in turn.

Finally, Y'Godda spoke. "There is only one rightful owner to this banner."

Oh, thank the gaming gods, I thought. He was going to let me have it.

The spirit said, "This banner was meant to rally my troops during times of great strife, and it served me well."

Until it got him killed, I thought. According to gaming lore Y'Godda overextended his troops and was overrun by some troll army. Not that I was going to point this out to him now.

"It was meant to be used in war," he said.

Uh-oh, I thought.

"And therefore, can only be claimed in battle," he continued.

Double uh-oh.

He raised his hands and grinned at us. "If you both wish to make a claim for my banner, then there is only one way you can earn it."

The light in the cavern brightened, and Y'godda seemed to grow in size with his proclamation.

"You both must go to the Battle Field!"

The brightness grew until the world around me became a white void. Things were about to change, and in a big way.

"Oh, FILTERED," I said.

# CHAPTER TWO

My view-screen went completely white.

As I waited impatiently my thoughts went to Amara and what she'd done. My anger toward her grew. She'd used me to try to obtain the banner. Had she been stalking me, shadowing me while I worked my way through the quest chain?

Or maybe it was as simple as her waiting outside the sealed cavern until someone came along who had the ability to open it.

Regardless. Now, because of her, my chance to complete the quest had been delayed, if not outright stolen. Whatever was in store for me, I had to win. I couldn't let that thieving elf get the better of me.

A system message appeared before my vision.

*Entering Battle Field.*

I grimaced with disappointment. Battle Fields were not my favorite activity in the game. In fact, up until now, I'd never once ventured into one. Delving into the role-playing aspect of this universe was why I played, not for war games.

The message continued.

*Objective: Retrieve your opponent's banner and bring it to the Battle Field's center platform. The first player to keep their opponent's banner on the platform for five continuous minutes wins.*

*Note: Only players can take or return a banner.*

*Use resources to build a base to defend your banner. Assemble offensive units to help you capture the opponent's banner.*

A feeling of dread washed over my like ice water. This was something I didn't have any experience with, commanding armies or defending bases. I'd gone through my entire game playing existence as a solo player. Participating in group quests, sure. But actually commanding, or strategizing? Not my style.

This didn't look good for my prospects of winning. How much experience did Amara have with these?

*If units are eliminated, they can be replaced if you have the resources to do so. If you die, your avatar will be resurrected at your crypt.*

That, at least, was good news and an aspect of the Battle Fields I was aware of. Upon death, you did not get sent to the newbie zone at level one. You could continue on until the battle was finally finished.

A line up of humanoids appeared before me.

*Choose the race of your army. Each race has advantages and disadvantages, so choose wisely.*

Choose wisely? I thought. I don't even know what I'm doing!

Sighing, I called up the information on the first race, a troll.

Tall, green and with long gangly limbs, it certainly wasn't pretty. But was it a good Battle race?

*Race: Troll*

*Hit Points: 100*

*Speed: 25*

*Racial Notes: +10% speed when using mounts. Takes +15% additional damage from fire attacks.*

*Worker Notes: +5% to stone gathering.*

*Defensive Notes: None.*

*Attack Notes: +10% damage when using spears.*

I'll be honest, I didn't quite know what to think of this information. These statistics were an extremely simplified version of what you would see in the gaming universe, itself. But here, in the Battle Fields, many stats were missing, like Intelligence or Strength. Which was fine. These weren't the same kind of Non-Player Characters you would normally find. These were pawns in a game of violent chess. It wasn't the tiny details which would make or break them it was how they were used overall.

I pulled up the Ogre figure. Tall, wide and brutish, it looked like something I would not want to face while questing, let alone on a battlefield.

*Race: Ogre*

*Hit Points: 150*

*Speed: 10*

*Racial Notes: +15% damage in melee combat. Cannot use mounts of any kind. +15% damage taken by fire attacks.*

*Worker Notes: +10% to stone gathering.*

*Defensive Notes: +5% damage when close to a Unit Leader.*

*Attack notes: +20% damage to walls or other base structures.*

Wow. Ogres, with their bonuses made them the tanks of the battle ground. But their lack of speed, coupled with no mounted units - which meant no cavalry - sucked big time.

Next was the Goblin race, who looked like a smaller version of the troll, only slightly less hideous.

*Race: Goblin*

*Hit Points: 85*

*Speed: 25*

*Racial Notes: +10% damage bonus when using spears. +15% chance to avoid arrow attacks. +20% damage taken against fire.*

*Worker Notes: -5% to stone & wood gathering.*

*Defensive Notes: +10% to morale when near another army unit.*

*Attacking Notes: +15% speed when using mounts. +5% accuracy with archer ability.*

Small, fast, but with crappy hit points. The hit to the resource gathering was glaring. From what little I knew of Battle Fields, this game was about resources. The more you had the better your ability to create defenses and units.

I scratched Goblins of my list.

Next was the elf. Thin to the point of being reed-like, it had long flowing hair and stared pensively into the distance.

*Race: Elf*

*Hit Points: 100*

*Speed: 25*

*Racial Notes: +15% accuracy, +15% speed when using mounts.*

*Worker Notes: +10% to wood gathering.*

*Defensive Notes: +20% morale when defending the banner. +10% chance to avoid arrow attacks. Cannot use heavy armor.*

*Attacking Notes: +15% to accuracy when near a forest tile. +10% damage with archery. Cannot use heavy weapons.*

Light-footed and good with bows. Not surprising. The wood gathering bonus was nice, but the lack of any heavy armored units was a let down.

The last selection was Human.

*Race: Human*

*Hit Points: 100*

*Speed: 20*

*Racial Notes: +10% damage bonus when using bows. +5 morale boost when near a Unit Leader.*

*Worker Notes: +10% to stone gathering. +10% to wood gathering.*

*Defensive Notes: +10% morale when defending the banner.*

*Attacking Notes: +5% to melee damage. +5% Hit Points to structures. +10% damage taken when attacked by fire.*

Perhaps because my avatar was human, I liked what I saw. The bonus to melee damage and structures looked great. But what really got my attention was the advantages with resources gathering.

If I was going to flail around trying to learn how to command an army, I needed all the resources I could get (and potentially squander).

Selecting Human was a no-brainer for me.

*Race selected.*

I wondered which Amara had chosen.

Then it asked:

*If you would like to send a message to your opponent, do so now.*

Huh, I didn't quite know what to say that didn't involve cursing, so I just sent: *That banner is mine!*

Yeah, lame, I know.

Amara responded with: *Eat FILTERED, you FILTERing FILTERED!*

Charming.

Then my view-screen cleared again, the line of races vanishing. A message appeared which made my heart race with anticipation.

*Prepare For Battle!*

# CHAPTER THREE

*You Have Entered The Battle Field.*

The white void which enveloped me dissolved into a picturesque landscape.

I stood on a grassy plain. The blue sky above was dotted with white puffy clouds. A breeze tugged at my cloak. This was no longer the cavern.

The plain which stretched off in all directions, was encompassed by a forest, thickly packed with trees almost resembling a green wall. Beyond, on all sides, were high vaulted cliffs.

The only direction that did not have these imposing cliffs was north. At first glance it appeared the forest thinned out to the northeast and northwest.

There was another aspect I took immediate note of.

I was completely alone. No army, no buildings, no base, no anything. It would appear I would be starting from scratch.

It was then I noticed I held a wooden pole which was topped with a flowing banner. It looked identical to the Lost War Banner of Y'Godda, only its color was red.

I looked at my cloak and leather armor. They, too, were the same deep red coloring.

Guess I'm team red, I thought, glancing around with confusion. But what do I do now? And where was Amara?

As if sensing my thoughts, the game brought up a small rectangular map which appeared at the top right of my view-screen. Near its bottom, surrounded by a mass of dark trees was a tiny red icon.

Me.

Okay. This was the map of the Battle Field. I was at the south end so I could assume Amara was standing, holding a banner, at its top northern end.

A system message appeared.

*Amara Frostwalker has placed her banner.*

I frowned up at mine. Where to put it?

I gave the map another look. If Amara was going to be attacking from the north, then I needed to keep as far back to the south as I could get.

The southern part of the plain ended at the tree line forming a natural cul de sac. I'd set up at the back and work from there.

I jogged south about a hundred paces feeling like I was just wasting time, now that Amara had begun building the apparatus which would potentially bring about my destruction.

Now, now, I admonished myself. An able commander must always be optimistic. No one else would be.

I stopped about thirty paces from the trees and gave my domain the once over. Seemed as good a place as any.

Gripped firmly in both hands, I brought the end of the banner's wooden pole down into the ground.

Instantly the earth boiled, forcing me to stumble backward.

From the roiling earth emerged skeletons.

My sword appeared in my hand as I looked at these undead apparitions with alarm.

Almost a dozen of the things forced their way up out of the ground, but none gave me the slightest bit of attention. Crawling over one another they each reached forward with a hand and grasped the banner's pole.

Then they all went still.

I blinked at this strange sight. In a macabre form of an altar, the skeletons had created the base from which my red banner fluttered.

Then a large shaft of light fell upon the banner and its grotesque keepers. The light formed a column that reached up into the sky, shifting like a curtain and glowing brightly.

I stepped back, head craned up to look at this bright column. Like a spotlight. Then a thought hit me.

I spun around and looked north.

There, far in the distance, well beyond the trees, like a golden thread but still noticeable, was another column of light that stretched up into the sky.

The location of Amara's banner.

Be seeing you soon, I thought.

A new icon shaped like a shield flashed at the left of my view-screen. Selecting it brought up a menu with various selections.

*Command Menu:*

*Build Keep: 1,000 gold, 300 stone, 150 wood (upgradeable)*

*Other Buildings: (Keep required)*

*Build Woodyard: 200 gold, 100 wood*

*Build Quarry: 200 gold, 150 wood*

*Build Goldmine: 200 gold, 150 wood*

*Build Barracks: 350 gold, 200 wood*

*Upgrade Keep: 3,500 gold, 1000 stone, 600 wood.*

I frowned at my selection. Was I to use my own gold to make the initial purchases? That didn't make sense, but no one said this game had to be fair, either.

A loud clinking of metal drew my attention back to the banner's skeletal altar. A large sack was held up by a pair of bony hands.

Okay, then. I approached to find the sack was partially open. Gold coins glittered within. My start up fund.

When I grabbed the sack, it vanished, and the hands holding it curled into fists. Suddenly, a status line appeared at the top of my view screen.

*Gold x 2,000 – Stone x 0 – Wood x 0*

Sweet, I thought. The keep was needed to start this party, but I lacked the wood and stone resources. I looked to the nearby tree line. Hacking at the trees with my sword didn't seem plausible. Then I noticed there were other items being held by the skeletal hands of the banner's altar.

One grasped a thick tree branch. Another held a large stone as if ready to throw it.

With some hesitation I took the branch, and the hand curled into a fist. The branch dissolved into a thousand moths that fluttered away in the breeze.

My status line updated.

*Gold x 2,000 – Stone x 0 – Wood x 500*

Next, I snatched the stone out of the other hand's grasp, but as it curled into a fist, its middle finger remained pointed upward.

Same to you buddy, I thought.

The stone cracked like an egg in my hand, and dozens of little gray lizards squirmed out to fall to the ground. They quickly buried themselves into the dirt and were gone.

Another status line update.

*Gold x 2,000 – Stone x 450 – Wood x 500*

Now we're in business. Flush with gold and resources I brought up the command menu and selected the Build Keep option. An information screen floated before me.

*Keep:*

*The key building of your base, it is required to construct other buildings. It is also required for hiring Worker Units. Worker Units can construct buildings.*

*Cost: 1,000 Gold + 300 Stone + 150 Wood.*

*Do you wish to purchase this building? Yes/No?*

But what if I didn't have any workers to build the keep in the first place? The chicken before the egg syndrome.

Only one way to find out, I thought, with a shrug and selected Yes.

A clattering of bones gave me a start.

From the banner's base, a tall skeleton emerged from the ground and stood before me. Cupped in its hands, causing it to stoop with its weight, was a large block of stone.

I blinked in surprise at this new arrival. Very cool, if not a bit creepy.

The skeleton's jaw worked open and closed. A voice slithered in my ear.

*Where?*

I repressed the urge to tell it to put the block anywhere just to get rid of the undead thing. But a strategic spot needed to be found. Everything I built should also be placed to impede an attacking force from getting to the banner.

I walked fifteen paces directly north of the banner's altar, then pointed at the spot between my feet. To the skeleton, I said, "Here, please."

The thing moved to the indicated spot, waddling under the weight of the block. As it approached, I took a few steps backward.

The skeleton stopped right on the spot and froze. It turned its skull to face in my direction.

The voice returned to squirm in my ear.

*Back.*

Not wanting to hear it speak again, I moved all the way back to the altar.

Once I was clear, the skeleton dropped the block to the ground with a dull thud. Then the bones of the undead apparition became unhinged and fell apart into a heap. The bones crumbled away into dust.

The upright stone block shimmered, then began to grow bigger and bigger. As it ballooned in size, a progress meter appeared next to it. *15%. 22%. 35%.*

As it got larger, so did the number on the progress meter. The block began to change shape, forming a squat tower.

At 100% the tower stopped growing and a system message appeared.

*Keep construction completed.*

I marveled at this new structure. It was about three stories high and about ten paces in diameter. Stone battlements ringed its crown and arrow slits dotted its surface at different levels.

And it was mine!

A large wooden door was at its base, facing south.

Maybe I'll go inside and look around my new keep, I thought.

But before I even moved, the door flew open and people spilled out of it. So surprised, I jumped back, sword in hand.

As the last person exited the Keep, the door slammed shut.

Twelve men stood before me in two neat rows of six. Each were identical to the others, with a mat of dark hair and a mustache. They also wore a pair of dirty overalls with a red shirt underneath – my banner color. Some held hammers, others axes or hand saws. A single name card appeared above the group. Worker Unit.

They all looked expectantly at me.

"Uh, hello," I said for lack of anything else to say.

One of the workers stepped forward, and a small flowing red banner appeared above his head. The unit's leader.

"Whatcha want us to build, boss?" the leader asked.

Good question. Now that I had workers it was time to put them to constructing the next building.

Making the Keep took nearly all my gold and resources, but was a necessity. So I pointed at the line of trees to the south and said, "Cut those down and get me more wood."

The unit leader scratched his head. "Gonna need a woodyard first, boss. Can't do much without one, afraid to say."

Right. Woodyard. I selected it from my command menu.

*Woodyard:*

*Required to receive and process chopped wood into building materials and for other usable products like weapons.*

*Cost: 200 gold + 100 wood.*

*Do you wish to purchase this building? Yes/No?*

I selected Yes.

The worker leader perked up. "Right on, boss! Where do you want it?"

I pointed at a spot about ten paces from the southern tree line. As I did so an outline of a red square appeared on the ground. When I moved my finger, the outline skipped along with it. I settled the outline onto the spot I wanted and said, "Build it there."

The outline froze into place, and I lowered my hand.

"Let's do this, men!" shouted the unit leader, and the workers rushed over to the woodyard outline. They spaced themselves around the outline's perimeter and began to hammer and saw at it. The noise of their tools echoed off the trees.

From the ground a small log warehouse began to slowly emerge from the ground. Its progress indicator increased rapidly and in moments it was at 100%.

*Woodyard completed.*

The workers let out a brief cheer and wiped sweat from their brows. Then the unit leader pointed at the trees. "Time to chop wood!" he shouted. The tools in their hands changed to axes, and they each attacked a tree with gusto.

I caught myself grinning at them. Despite my initial trepidation I thought this was actually kind of fun.

With a little time to get the hang of things, I could get my base built, raise an army, and get Amara's banner.

How hard could that really be?

A shout pulled me out of my thoughts and I looked to the source.

At the top of the keep, leaning over the battlements, was a soldier clad in light armor. The indicator 'Lookout' was above his head. He pointed to the northwest. "Enemy spotted!" He shouted.

Shocked, I looked to where he pointed.

A large group of humanoids were running across the grass plains directly at me. They were tall, green and armed with spears. Each wore basic trousers and a simple blue colored jerkin.

Trolls.

Behind them, mounted on a sparkling white horse, was Amara. Even from this distance I could see her grin.

The trolls were approaching at an alarming speed, such was their racial advantage.

I found myself paralyzed with indecision. I had no soldiers or defenses and was about to be hit with what many players considered the most notorious tactic in a Battle Field game.

A grunt rush.

# CHAPTER FOUR

Faced with little choice I decided to engage the enemy full on. Once within my base's perimeter they would slaughter the workers and raze the Keep. And worst of all, the banner would be lost.

I had to stop them, but doing so on foot would be folly.

*Summon Shadow Steed.*

A magnificent black horse with full rider's tack appeared before me. He nickered in greeting. This was my mount, Smoke.

I leapt up into his saddle and kicked him forward. As we closed the distance with the approaching trolls, I pulled up their stats.

*Unit: Foot Soldiers*

*Battle Rank: Grunt*

*Hit Points: 100*

*Speed: 25*

*Main Weapon: Spear*

A quick count told me that there were twelve trolls all together, with Amara as their back up. She'd pulled this tactic as a way to overrun my defenseless base and grab the banner. Never mind a long protracted battle, she was going for the quick and easy victory.

I found myself getting pretty angry and summoned my bow with a quiver of arrows. Several volleys into the grunts scored hits, but I had an accuracy penalty while riding so fast.

With neither the trolls nor I altering our course, I charged straight into them. At the last second I switched to my sword and swung at the nearest grunt. I sliced the top of his spear off and followed through to lop off his head.

A system message appeared.

*You have killed a grunt. +1 Battle Points.*

*You have gained 125 experience points toward your next level.*

The status bar at the top of my view expanded to include a new indicator. *Battle Points: 1.*

But I barely noticed any of this, caught up in the heat of combat.

As the grunt's corpse fell to the ground, the other trolls ran right past, without trying to engage me at all. Their target was obvious: my workers, who blissfully chopped away at the trees.

I yanked at Smoke's reigns to bring him around and swung at the head of the nearest troll.

*You have killed a grunt. +1 Battle Points.*

*You have gained 125 experience points toward your next level.*

A sudden pain pierced my lower back, and I looked around.

Amara grinned at me as she nocked another arrow in her bow. She kept her distance to get better aim at me.

Two can play at this game, I thought. I switched to my bow and fired at her, but she easily dodged it.

"Think you got what it takes to beat me, FILTERED?" Amara shouted.

I was about to send Smoke into a full charge but pulled up short. This was what Amara wanted, to keep me busy and draw me away from my base.

Instead of taking the bait, I turned Smoke south and kicked him into a full gallop directly at the grunt unit. Behind me I heard Amara cursing, but I ignored her.

By now the trolls had entered the defensive perimeter of the keep. The Lookout was firing a bow at them but with little effect. He appeared to be the Keep's only defender.

I shouted a warning to the workers, who all turned to gape at their inbound executioners.

The lead troll ran up to the closest worker and ran him through with a spear. The worker dropped his axe and fell over dead.

At that moment I charged into the backs of the trolls, swinging wildly. Two died in moments and were added to my Battle Points.

But my workers were dying left and right, felled by spears.

Suddenly, the trolls changed their attention from the frightened workers to target me.

Spears jabbed at Smoke's side and I managed to batter some attacks away. The quick change caught me off guard but I recovered and pushed Smoke out of their midst.

As I lopped the head off of another troll, I caught movement out of the corner of my eye.

Amara was charging past the keep, the Lookout feebly firing arrows at her. She wasn't coming to save her grunts, or attack me.

She was going for the banner!

I tried to move to cut her off, but the grunts surrounded me again, spears jabbing. With frustration I shouted at the worker unit's leader. "Get to the banner! Defend the banner!"

The leader blinked at me in disbelief, then held up his axe. He pointed toward the banner altar and yelled. "To the banner, boys!"

The surviving workers ran toward the altar which they were much closer to than Amara.

I knew I'd just sent them to their doom, but I needed time.

Smoke suddenly kicked backward sending a troll smashing against a tree.

*+1 Battle Points.*

With more frantic swings of my sword, I managed to push us through the grunts. With a final decapitation, I ran at the banner's altar.

The remaining workers, totaling six, arrived at the altar just as Amara did. They swung their axes but did almost no damage to her or her mount.

Finding them more of an annoyance, she tried to knock them aside with her horse. The workers only got in the way, slowing her down.

Close enough now to grab the banner, she reached out a hand.

My heart sank in my chest.

But the worker's leader smacked her hand away with his axe, causing her to nearly lose her balance. She screamed with rage.

Then I slammed into her side at a full charge.

Amazingly, she recovered from this sudden assault and parried my sword swings. Her white horse kicked, and a worker pinwheeled away.

With an effort, I placed myself between her and the banner, our swords clashing. She was highly skilled with melee weapons, I gave her that, but kept up my attack.

The remaining troll grunts, three in all, joined the fray. Amara grinned, knowing I would be overwhelmed. Sweat dripped down my forehead as I now had to contend with four different attackers.

With only four workers as my defense force, I commanded them to concentrate on a single troll who's health indicator showed to be the weakest of the three.

But the two other trolls pressed their attack, spears thrusting at me. One pierced Smoke's side and my mount reared in pain, nearly throwing me off. But as the horse landed, he struck out with his forelegs and crushed a troll who stepped in for a killing blow.

*+1 Battle Points.*

As this was happening, Amara pushed in toward the altar, and this time grabbed onto the banner by its long wooden handle.

A system message practically screamed across my screen.

*Your Banner Has Been Taken!*

Amara yanked upward, but, dodging a spear thrust, I swung my sword around in a wide arc and connected with her shoulder.

*Swords Skill Increased! Level 9, 73%*

She screamed in pain and let go of the banner.

*Your Banner Has Been Returned!*

The elven Shadow pulled her mount around to face off with me, sword in hand.

*+1 Battle Points.*

I didn't kill anyone at that moment, and a quick glance told me that one of the trolls had been slain, but at the cost of two workers. The worker leader stood over the corpse of the troll, looking triumphant.

The last troll, taking advantage of my distraction, deeply speared my left side. My avatar gasped in pain, and blood flowed freely from the wound.

Not good, I thought with alarm as my health bar dropped.

In that instant Amara was one me. She swung her sword with an almost maniacal glee, sensing victory was at hand.

It took every thing I had to parry her blows, but my avatar was weakening from the bleeding wound.

Quickly, I opened my avatar's inventory and selected a stack of Health Potions to drink. These would bring up my hit points to 100% in an instant.

But when I tried to use the Health Potion, a red system message appeared.

*Not a Battle Field item. Cannot be used.*

What the heck? I thought while dodging a spear thrust.

I tried to use a Health Potion, again, but the same message appeared.

A cry of anguish pulled me back into the situation.

Amara had switched to her bow and shot the worker leader through the head as he tried running at her.

Rage overtook me. With a determined focus, I smacked away the last troll's spear thrust and jammed my sword through its throat. It collapsed to the ground.

*+1 Battle Points.*

*You have gained 125 experience points toward your next level.*

Amara backed her mount away a few paces from me, a victorious grin plastered across her smug face. "Got any final words, FILTERED?" she said raising her bow to aim at me.

I'd maneuvered myself between her and the banner's altar. With one hand covering the bleeding wound in my side, I knew the writing was on the wall.

"Yeah," I said with a smile. "Give up now and I will show you mercy."

Amara cackled. "You got quite the mouth on you. Had I known you were a Battle Field noob, I would have waited a while longer before crushing you. Built a full army and then marched over the ruins of your base."

As she spoke, I noticed a system message at the bottom of my screen. It was marked as a non-priority. When I brought it up, it caused me to catch my breath.

*Your only Worker Unit has been eliminated. Do you wish to purchase another – Cost 100 gold? Yes/No?*

"Oh, heck, yeah!" I blurted.

Amara's triumphant expression flickered with confusion. "What are you talking about? You want me to crush you?"

"Yes," I said with a widening smile.

*Worker Unit purchased.*

Suddenly, the door to the Keep flew open and a dozen new workers spilled out in a rush.

Amara shifted her focus from me to the new arrivals and fired her bow at them. One of the workers died from the shot.

Immediately, I pointed at Amara and shouted, "Get her!"

The eleven remaining workers turned their heads in unison to look at Amara. Axes appeared in their hands which they raised with a cheer, then charged.

Amara barked a laugh as she shot and killed another worker. "This is pathetic," she said. "You are just delaying the inevitable, you stupid FILTERED."

She was right, I thought. But only partially.

I summoned a Magma arrow which appeared in my quiver. At close quarters, I hadn't bothered using my bow against Amara. She was too fast, and the game penalized range attacks within a short distance. But now an opportunity presented itself.

The worker unit massed around her, commanding her attention. For whatever reason, she didn't run away, or try to get distance from them. Instead, she switched to her sword and hacked at her feeble attackers.

Ignoring various '*You are bleeding out!*' health warnings, I took aim and fired.

Amara must have sensed the attack coming. As she cut the head off of a determined worker, she looked over at me.

The magma arrow hit her right in the sternum, piercing her chest. Instantly, she dropped her sword and her avatar screamed in pain. Her screams turned into a hellish gurgling sound.

I knew what was about to happen and commanded the workers to fall back, which they did.

Amara fell from her horse and spasmed on the ground. From her mouth and ears gushed hot lava. It melted her face away in an instant and soon bubbled over her entire body.

In seconds, Amara's avatar had been rendered down to a bubbling puddle of magma. Her horse turned and ran away in fright.

A system message appeared.

*Vivian Valesh has killed Amara Frostwalker. +1,000 Battle Points.*

The workers let out a cheer, but I wasn't feeling particularly victorious. Yes, I had killed her, but she'd be back once she resurrected at a crypt.

The only way to win this battle field was with her banner.

Still, at least I prevented her from stealing an early victory with a grunt rush tactic.

I pushed these thoughts from my mind. My avatar's health dropped further and the image on my view-screen wavered.

Crap, I thought. I can't die now. Amara would get a thousand battle points! She didn't deserve that!

I suddenly found myself on the ground, Smoke looking down on me with equine concern.

If I can't use my Health Potions in the battle field, how in the heck am I expected to survive very long?

As my screen darkened I heard the Lookout shout from high above.

"Get the Commander inside! Quickly!"

Hands lifted me and I could make out motion on my screen. Was I being moved?

As I prepared for a trip to the nearest crypt, a system message appeared.

*Amara Frostwalker has been reborn to the world. The battle continues!*

Figures, I thought.

Then the world went dark.

# CHAPTER FIVE

*You Have Been Rendered Unconscious.*

Oh great, I thought as I glared at my black screen. It would be better if my avatar died now so that I could pop up at a crypt and get back to building my base. And this time I'd get my own grunts, and fast!

I didn't think I'd survive another grunt rush. It was hard to tell if Amara would attempt one again. She needed to call up a new unit of grunts, but I didn't know if she had the resources to do it immediately.

It would help if I knew more about this Battle Field game. I inwardly cursed myself for never learning this aspect of the gaming universe. I'd certainly explored the rest, but war games were never of interest to me. Questing was.

Now I had to learn, and quick. Amara could not be allowed to win and be awarded the Lost War Banner of Y'Godda. It would mess up my quest chain I'd struggled so hard through.

And then there was the final reward for returning the banner to the quest giver.

Frustrated waiting for my inevitable death, I pulled up my inventory again. I didn't have a proper chance to look at it more closely while fighting Amara.

All the items my avatar carried were grayed out. I couldn't select any of them. Health Potions. Maps. Items. Nothing.

The only things I could access were some skills, weapons and armor. The last was quite fortunate as it allowed me to continue to use my legendary Cloak of Shadows, but not all of its myriad of benefits. No phase, or invisibility, or teleportation. Sheesh. Why don't they just take away all the fun?

Out of all my special gadgets and trick arrows, only the magma arrow was available.

My view-screen began to brighten, and the darkness faded. The health indicator at the edge of my vision began to rise at a wonderfully quick rate. Was a healer attending to my wounds?

When I could see fully again, I found myself face down on a cold stone floor. With a groan from my avatar I rolled over and sat up.

I was in the Keep, its circular stone walls stretching above me. A narrow stone stairway spiraled up its length until it reached the wooden roof and ended at an open trap door. Through the door was a face peering down at me. The Lookout.

There was nothing else here. No furnishings or other exits save the one wooden door.

The worker leader knelt beside me. When I sat up his face changed from deep concern to elation.

"Thank Y'Godda, you are okay!" he said and danced a happy jig.

I laughed at the odd sight and got to my feet. Although my balance was a little off, it improved as my health bar increased.

"How did you heal me?" I asked. "I was surely going to die." I looked at my side where the spear at almost gutted me, but there was no wound. Even my light armor had mended itself.

The leader said, "The Commander of Red can find a second chance here in the Keep. Y'godda has blessed it. May he be praised!"

I nodded. Being inside the Keep granted health regeneration. Interesting. "Yes, may he be praised," I said. I expected Amara to already be aware of this fact, unfortunately. This just underscored my woeful lack of Battle Field knowledge.

"Thank you, for bringing me inside," I said.

The leader shrugged. "Weren't nothing, boss. It was the Lookout's idea, after all."

I looked up again and waved at the Lookout who returned it. Then he vanished from view and back to his duties.

And speaking of which, I had duties, too. Build a base, and an army and then smash Amara's face in. I liked that plan.

The leader asked, "What is your command, boss? Me and the lads are waiting." He motioned toward the door where a cluster of workers stared at me in anticipation.

"Right," I said, and headed to the door. The workers scattered.

Outside, they assembled themselves into two neat rows.

As soon as I crossed the Keep's threshold my hit point regeneration stopped. I stepped back inside the doorway and surveyed my meager base. All the dead bodies had vanished.

Smoke grazed next to the banner's altar, and I was relieved to see he had recovered from his wounds.

The woodyard stood abandoned with only a tiny bit of wood piled inside it. I'd need them to start cutting wood, again. Then find a gold mine and begin to dig.

It was going to be a lot of work. I eyed the worker unit who were missing a few men. I'd need more workers than this lot. A lot more.

"Where can I get more of you?" I asked the leader.

He waved at the Keep. "Why, from there, boss. You can have thirty six stalwart workers at this level. More when you upgrade it."

Thirty six workers meant three units. On a hunch I pulled up my command menu again and highlighted the Keep.

*Keep:*

*Hire Worker Unit – 100 gold (1/3 units active)*

Feeling pressed for time, I selected to hire another worker unit. The upgrade option would have to wait.

Instantly, the round room of the Keep was filled with twelve burly workers in overalls and red shirts. This unit's leader stepped forward.

"What would you like us to do, boss?" he said. He looked and sounded identical to the one outside.

I shrugged inwardly. Well, they're only workers. Don't need to tell them apart.

"Outside, please," I said.

The streamed past me through the door and assembled next to the other unit.

My health bar was now full, all hit points restored. I marveled at how close I'd come to giving that elven idiot a thousand battle points with my death and laughed. She must be steaming right now.

No, I corrected myself. Not steaming. Building. And fast.

I stepped through the door and pointed at the first worker unit. Each one stood at attention like soldiers on parade.

"Resume cutting wood over there, please," I said indicating the tree line by the woodyard.

"Yes, boss!" the leader screamed, and they all turned in unison and ran off. In seconds they were chopping away as if possessed.

"And us, boss?" the leader of the new unit asked.

I liked their eagerness but interacting with them could eventually get on my nerves. Instead of answering, I pulled up the command menu and selected the Build Barracks option.

*Barracks:*

*Needed to muster and train various battle units.*

*Cost: 350 gold, 200 wood*

*Do you wish to build this? Yes/No?*

Selecting yes produced a large rectangular outline on the ground. I pointed it toward a spot right beside the banner's altar.

"Build me a barracks there, please," I said.

The worker unit sprang into action, surrounding the outline and hammering away. A long narrow building with many windows slowly emerged from the ground. Next to it looked to be a small parade ground for marching and wooden dummies for fighting practice.

Completed, the workers stopped and wiped their sweaty brows, but they still glanced at me with expectation.

My gold was seriously depleted so I wouldn't be able to build anything for a while.

I pointed to the woodyard. "Go help them out."

With the leader shouting at them, they took off to attack the trees.

Two system messages appeared.

*Archery Range unlocked.*

*Cavalry Grounds unlocked.*

Cool, I thought, but blanched when I saw their prices.

*Archery Range: 700 gold, 200 wood*

*Cavalry Grounds: 1,000 gold, 200 wood*

Won't be getting those for a while.

Instead, I brought up the command screen and selected the new Barracks submenu.

*Barracks:*

*Units available:*

*Footmen – 200 gold.*

*Scout – 50 gold.*

Looking at my resources I had enough for one of each. I selected the footmen first.

*Race: Human*

*Unit: Footmen*

*Hit Points: 100*

*Speed: 20*

*Weapon: Sword*

*Although slow, Footmen are the most common type of combat unit for both attacking and defending.*

In terms of statistics, they looked identical to the troll grunts. I assumed all soldier units across the races were more or less even.

*Train this unit? Cost 200 gold. Yes/No?*

I selected yes, and a dozen men appeared in the training yard. Each wore basic cloth armor with a red jerkin. Armed with swords, some stabbed at the training dummies while others sparred on the parade grounds. A unit leader screamed a stream of filtered profanities at them.

*Time to train unit: 5 minutes.*

Oh, yeah. This stuff takes time, I thought with mild disappointment.

While I waited for my first combat unit to finish training, I called up the Scout's info.

*Race: Human*

*Unit: Scout*

*Hit Points: 85*

*Speed: 30*

*Weapon: Bow & dagger*

*The scout is best used to seek out resources and monitor for enemy movements. Gains a +20% camouflage bonus when moving through trees.*

This was what I needed. I'll use the scout to look for resources while I attended to a certain matter.

But when I tried to purchase the scout unit, I got a message.

*Can only train one unit at a time, per barracks. Add Scout to training queue? Yes/No?*

Heck, yes.

*Scout added.*

I frowned at the message. Only one unit at a time meant I'd need more than one barracks if I wanted to push out multiple units quickly.

A shout from the tree line brought me out of my contemplations.

For a moment, I thought another grunt rush was underway, and even summoned my bow.

One of the leaders ran over to me, beaming with excitement.

"Boss! We found a stone just inside the tree line," he said panting with breath.

"Let's take a look," I said.

We hurried over to where the workers were feverishly cutting away. Tree stumps showed their rapid progress, and the woodyard had a growing pile of cut lumber.

"Over here," said the leader, pointing.

I picked my way through the trees and noted how close they were to one another. Like a living fence, an army would not be able to slink their way through without being slowed to a crawl.

Then a clearing opened up amongst the densely packed trees. The entire space was composed of an outcropping of layered stone.

I looked at it blankly. "This is the stone we need?"

The leader nodded. "Yes, boss. Y'Godda smiles upon us placing it so close to the Keep."

"Well, thank Y'Godda, then," I said. From my command menu I purchased a quarry with the last of my gold. Then I placed its outline on the flattest portion of the rocks. I told the leader to stop cutting trees and bring his unit over to assemble the quarry and start cutting stone.

He nodded happily, then screamed for his men.

Leaving them to it, I walked back through the tree line to the Keep. Smoke wandered over and nuzzled me hand.

That was the quarry taken care of, but without any more gold, nothing else would be built and no more units could be trained. I had to find a vein of gold and fast.

*Footmen Unit training complete.*

I looked toward the barracks.

The soldiers I'd seen training on the grounds had assembled themselves next to the barracks building in two rows of six with their leader at the front end.

*Scout Unit in training.*

A solitary man, clad in leather armor with a deep green hooded cloak skulked around the training grounds. He shot at one of the dummies with a bow, then quickly stabbed another with a dagger.

*Time to train unit: 2 minutes.*

The footmen leader suddenly bellowed, "Ready for orders, Commander!"

I walked along the assembled lines of men, making a show of inspecting them. If I was expected to command them, then I could pretend to act like I knew what I was doing.

Each man gave me a slight head nod as I passed.

To the leader I said, "I have a very important task for you."

"We are ready to do whatever you ask of us, Commander!" he said.

I nodded. "Our resources are depleted so I cannot afford more soldiers for a while. Can you split this unit into two groups?"

"Of course, Commander."

"Good. Please assign half your men to guard the workers over there at the trees."

"Yes, Commander!" the leader then barked orders at his unit. One row of six men broke rank and marched quickly over to stand near the woodyard.

I then pointed at the banner's skeletal altar. "Place the others there. They are to prevent anyone from touching the banner at all costs."

"Yes, Commander!" he said, followed be more barking of orders. With a nod, the leader trailed after his men and they formed a circle around the altar.

I tried not to get too depressed looking at my twelve footmen. This was all I had, and I knew it would not even be close to enough once Amara came calling again. And she would.

*Scout Unit training complete.*

The Scout jogged over to stand next to the barracks building. He leaned against his bow almost casually and gave me a slight nod. "Commander," he said. "What do you need of me?"

The cool loner type, I thought. "We need gold," I said and swung a hand to indicate the forest to the south. "I need you to go in there and find a vein of gold and report it to me immediately. In fact, report anything you find in there that might be useful."

I assumed that gold would be placed close to each opponent's starting area. But mine was not out in the open, so it must be in the trees somewhere. Or so I hoped.

No gold, no chance at victory.

The scout nodded again and skulked off toward the tree line. Within moments he vanished from view.

I surveyed my little empire. Few men, and even fewer resources did not bode well for a good start. And until there was actual gold to use there was little else for me to do here.

With a single leap I was back in Smoke's saddle. I pointed him northwest, the direction Amara and her grunts had appeared from, and kicked at his sides.

The footmen leader called out to me in alarm. "Commander! Where are you going?"

"Look after things while I'm gone," I shouted over me shoulder. "I think it's time I gave my opponent a little visit."

Then I broke into a gallop.

# CHAPTER SIX

I followed the open plains to the northwest until my base vanished from view behind the trees.

The terrain changed little; flat ground buttressed by tall trees on either side. The map began to fill out with these details and eventually showed that the plains curved around toward the north.

Other than the occasional flock of birds, and a mother boar with piglets which scampered through the forest, I encountered nothing else.

I'd assumed that Amara would have perhaps tried to send another grunt unit to attack again. No doubt, her resources were just as depleted as mine.

After investigating several blank patches of ground with exposed rock along the way, but finding no gold, I came to the conclusion any potential gold veins would be hidden. Or placed in strategic spots around the map.

Lost in thought, I almost didn't notice a slight change in the tree line to the east. There was a distinct gap with the beginnings of a narrow path.

Curious, I trotted over, wary of an ambush.

It was definitely a path, well worn. But it was far to narrow to ride Smoke through.

Where did this path lead and did Amara notice it when she passed this way before? Based on how fast she grunt-rushed me, I doubted she had time to investigate it herself.

I considered my options. Keep exploring north, or follow the path. A glance at the map, with icons representing each building and units, showed nothing had changed. The scout had traveled due south until he came upon the sheer barrier cliffs and turned northeastward. No indications of him discovering a gold vein.

Gold could be here though.

Not wanting to waste any more time, I dismounted. With a snap of my fingers Smoke popped out of existence and the mount icon on my view-screen went on a two-minute re-summoning timer.

I didn't think I'd need to run off in a hurry within the next two minutes. At least I hoped not.

Sword in hand, I entered the forest along the path. The air cooled around me so much I had to go into my game settings and reduce my simulation suit's temperature controls. I liked a good virtual reality experience as much as the next person, but I didn't need to freeze to death while doing so.

A few paces along, the gap behind me disappeared from view. Somewhere, deep within the crowd of dark trees came the ululating cries of some animal.

I paused, waiting. The cry came again, but further away. Without a clue as to what it was, I decided to take a precaution and slipped into Shadow Form. I effectively became invisible to a casual observer. And provided I stayed within shadows and did not engage in combat, my pseudo-invisibility would not negate. A unique ability given to the Shadow class.

I moved further inward following the path's twists and turns through the foliage. After several minutes I started to worry it may go on forever, or at least cut across the entire width of the map. There was no time for such folly.

I'd almost convinced myself to turn and go back when a chat request appeared on my view-screen. But unlike a player requesting a chat with their name attached to it, this one simply said, 'SCOUT'.

I selected the request, and a screen opened up before me. The cool gaze of the scout greeted me.

"Uh, hello, Scout," I said with hesitation. I'd never once received a chat request from a NPC before. And, to be quite honest, didn't know they even had the capability. Perhaps it was a feature only found in Battle Field sessions?

The scout nodded once, his hood pulled down low to almost cover his eyes. "Found you some gold, Commander." The screen angled away from him to show a wall of sheer rock. A wide spot along its dark surface glittered with gold, its veined pattern spreading outward like roots.

I felt a rush of relief at the sight. "Oh, thank the Gaming Gods!" I said.

The scout put the screen on him. "Gaming Gods, or Y'godda," he said with a shrug. "Who's to know which?"

I actually laughed at his odd humor. "Well, I thank them both. Can you lead some workers to that spot?"

"Not needed," the scout said. "It's marked on the map."

And so it was, a gold nugget icon at the very bottom of my map against the cliff line.

"Okay, please continue scouting the forest and see what else you can find. When you're finished with the east forest, scout out the western one, too."

The scout nodded and was about to turn away when I said. "Oh, and Mr. Scout."

He looked at me expectantly.

"Good job!" I said with smile.

One corner of the scout's mouth raised a little which I took for his version of a grin, then he closed the chat screen.

I looked to my status screen to see where things stood.

The wood situation was fine, so I opted to pull the worker unit from their chopping duties. I selected their icon from the map then tapped the gold vein icon, and a system message appeared

*Build a Gold Mine at this location? Cost: 200 gold, 150 wood - Yes/ No?*

"Heck, yeah!" I said.

Immediately, the worker unit's icon moved through the trees in the direction of the gold vein. It really annoyed me that I didn't even have the 100 gold to hire my third worker unit to help out. But such are things when you are just starting out. Later, I hoped to have dozens of these units toiling away on buildings, mines, and defenses.

A worry tickled the back of my brain. I selected the half unit of footmen which had been guarding the woodyard. Then I assigned them to the gold vein. They moved as well, a short distance behind the worker unit.

This meager defense of the gold mine would have to do for now. I was just grateful the thing actually existed.

Another quick glance at the map overview of the base showed nothing else of note. Workers chipped away in the quarry, and the other half unit of footmen stood guard at the banner's altar.

So if the gold mine is taken care of, did I still want to follow this path? Scouting north toward Amara's base seemed the more prudent use of my time.

But as I turned to go, something further down the path caught my eye.

Cautiously, I approached.

The path ended at a small open space between the trees. In the middle of this little clearing was a massive ogre.

He was kneeling, head bowed down. His wrists were shackled and bound by chains to giant iron loops in the ground.

His armor was patchwork, exposing acres of green skin crisscrossed with scars.

Now what do we have here? I thought. The being was easily taller than me while kneeling and as wide as a supply wagon.

I called up its information.

*Name: Grax*

*Unit: Champion*

*Race: Ogre*

*Hit Points: 500*

*Speed: 40*

*A former champion of Y'Godda's army.*

*Cost to free: 1,200 Battle Points.*

Whoa. Nice, but I couldn't afford him at the moment. I'd need to kill more trolls to get there first. Or Amara, again.

I chuckled at the last thought.

Hearing me, the ogre tilted his head up and looked around.

"Who is there?" Grax grumbled. His voice was deep and resonant.

Figuring I was safe while he was chained I slipped out of Shadow Form. "Hello," I said.

The humanoid regarded me, then nodded. "You are the red commander," he said. "Might you be here to free me from these chains?"

I shook my head. "Sorry, that'll have to wait a little while. Can't afford you."

Grax suddenly pulled violently at his chains, causing me to take a couple of steps back. Man, was he big.

"I will fight for you, Commander. Of that there is no doubt. Enemies with be crushed and victory will be yours with me at your side."

I held up a hand. "I don't need any convincing, my friend. My army is in desperate need of a champion such as yourself. But the time is not right. I do promise to return and free you from your bounds."

The green giant nodded. "I hope that you return soon. It has been ages since I've fought in battle and I crave the smell of blood and the sounds of agony!"

Laying it on a little thick, I thought. I'm already sold on him. Getting this guy on my side would be a priority. If for nothing more than to ensure Amara didn't get him first.

I said, "Worry not, Champion. Your time for killing is close at hand. I will return soon."

Before he could engage me with more of his sales pitch I waved and turned to leave.

"Blood and agony!" he bellowed. "The symphony of battle!"

Okay then, I thought and hurried back down the path.

A quick glance from the safety of the trees showed that the grassy plains were clear. I summoned Smoke and mounted up.

How many other Champions were hidden away on the map? With so much forest there could be several of them. And expensive to hire, too.

My attention went to my resource status line.

As I watched, the gold amount increased, making me smile. From my command menu I selected the Keep and bought my third unit of workers. Their icon instantly appeared by the Keep.

I then selected build Archery Range.

*Build Archery Range. Cost 700 gold, 200 wood – Yes/No?*

On a hunch I selected yes, and when I pointed at my map a tiny red square appeared. Perfect! I didn't have to be actually present at the base to build things. This undoubtedly was meant to free players to take to the field as opposed to staying holed up in their base mico-managing everything.

I placed the range next to the barracks and assigned the new worker unit to it.

Then, from the barracks menu, I selected to train another unit of footmen. Now all my money was gone, and I had to wait.

I called up the Keep info screen again and grimaced at its upgrade requirements. The stone needed was steep, yet, without the upgrade, I couldn't get more workers. I ordered the new worker unit to head to the quarry once the archery range was complete.

"By Y'Godda, it shall be done!" hollered the unit leader via chat with enthusiasm.

With my base management duties done for the moment, I turned Smoke north. We followed the curve of the plain's direction to the northeast until the trees on the northern side stopped.

Here, a wide river cut across the plains from west to east until it vanished into the forest on the opposite side.

Directly in its middle was a wide stone platform, which formed a kind of bridge across the water. An altar sat at its center.

This was where I had to bring Amara's banner.

Wary, I slowly approached. The flat ground I followed continued to the east then curved southward. On my map it looked like the southern section would make one big circle, with forest in the middle.

The scout suddenly reported in. "All done," he said, expression serious.

From the map I could tell there had been nothing of note in the remainder of the forest which partially encircled the base.

"Okay, go here, please." I tapped the forest line directly ahead of me, on the east side. "Stay hidden and watch for approaching enemies from the north."

This river appeared to be the middle choke point between the two halves of the map. Past the river, the forest resumed. Identical looking grassy plains curved northeast and northwest. The entire map must form a figure eight, with the river and platform at its middle.

When Amara or any of her units moved south, they'd have to cross here. Having the scout placed nearby would give me fair warning of the next attack.

The scout nodded once and closed the chat window. I shook my head. Having NPCs activate, and even terminate visual chats was new for me, and I can't say I was getting use to it.

As I got closer to the altar, its details became more clear. It was nearly identical to the one at my base, entangled skeletons with the top one extending an arm, waiting to grasp a banner.

The wide platform had no defenses. Bringing the banner here, let alone keeping it safe for five minutes, seemed a near impossible task. How could you defend it?

*Footmen Unit training complete.*

I smiled. That would do the trick.

With just enough gold, I started another unit to training. Then, selecting the new unit, I ordered them to move north to my position and guard the altar. I'd wait here until they arrived, then...

Movement to the northwest caught my eye.

A group of trolls were approaching on foot. But these weren't grunts. Workers.

As they got closer I could see they were wearing blue shirts under overalls. But their leggings only went down a little past their knees, giving them a comical look. Each held a hammer or axe.

A quick look beyond them, and to the northeast approach showed they were alone.

I laughed, and summoned my bow, waiting until they got within range.

"Easy pickings," I said with a smirk.

"I'll say!" came a shout from behind me.

I whirled to see Amara in mid-leap from atop the altar, descending upon me.

With no time to react I could only bring up my bow in a feeble attempt to block her sword.

But she crashed into me, driving her weapon straight through my chest. The force of the sudden attack knocked me off of Smoke, and I fell to the ground.

Flat on my back, my avatar had become paralyzed. I knew what this meant.

Amara bent over me, leering. "Payback's a FILTERED, ain't it, honey?" She wrenched the sword from my chest then turned her attention to poor Smoke.

As my screen darkened, I cursed myself for being so stupid. Then a message appeared before my vision.

*You Have Been Slain in Battle!*

Then my screen went black.

# CHAPTER SEVEN

*Amara Frostwalker has killed Vivan Valesh. +1,000 Battle Points for Amara Frostwalker.*

For several moments after my avatar's death, I yelled a stream of profanities with Amara's name attached to them, until I was blue in the face.

She'd hidden near the altar, probably under the platform itself, in Shadow Form. She knew that the approaching troll workers would probably distract me enough for her to sneak attack.

That's the second time she'd caught me off guard.

A thirty second timer counted down against the blackness of my view-screen. It was all I could do but glower at it.

A new system message appeared:

*Your Mount has been killed.*

More profanities, more glowering.

The thirty seconds felt like hours as adrenaline pulsed through my system. There was no doubt now that Amara had played a Battle Field session before. Possibly several.

And I was the Battle Field noob she got to toy with.

The counter reached zero and my screen brightened.

*Vivian Valesh has been reborn to the world. Let the Battle continue!*

My avatar was no longer at the middle, but was looking up at a low ceiling. I sat up to find I was on a raised stone slab in a cramped room. Fire sconces on the floor were the only source of light. Cob webs hung from the beams above and murals of battles draped across the stone walls.

A crypt.

An ascending stairway could be seen through the crypt's only door.

I stood and looked my avatar's body over. There was no sword wound in my chest and my cloak and cloth armor were undamaged. The health indicator on my screen showed my hit points at 100%. Nothing was missing from my inventory either (not that I could access it anyway).

Other than finding myself transported from the platform, there appeared to be no obvious death penalty.

Still, this beats a newbie zone, hands down.

I took the narrow stairs up to emerge from a floor into a tall round room made of stone blocks.

The Keep.

Far above, the Lookout waved through the trap door then returned to his duties.

Welcome home, I thought. Death was a quick trip back to base.

I stepped outside and squinted from the sunlight.

The archery range was complete. Several targets were lined up along the end of the range with a small stone building for housing archers at one side.

I pulled up its menu.

*Train Archer Unit: Cost 300 gold – Yes/No?*

Yes.

Several archers appeared on the range and shot arrows at the line of targets. Others stood to the side, fletching new arrows.

*Training time: five minutes.*

By now, there was enough gold for another unit of footmen so I started their training.

I frowned at my status line. Resources were not being collected even close to fast enough. If I wanted to begin an assembly line of troops, I'd need more workers and for that, a Keep upgrade.

The current bottle-neck was stone. Maybe if I took workers from...

*Enemy Contact!*

What?! I spun around looking for an enemy army rushing toward the base. Then my eyes were drawn to the map.

The footmen unit I'd assigned to the center altar was close to arriving at their destination. Two enemy grunt icons were now at the middle and moving to meet my lone unit.

I slapped my virtual forehead. I had completely forgotten about them, and now they were marching straight into trouble.

Panicking, I ordered the unit to stop, which they immediately did. But what to do with them? If I had them engage the enemy, they would be killed by overwhelming numbers. Plus, there were other enemy unit icons appearing from their north and heading toward the center platform.

But having them retreat wasn't an option either as they were now too close to the enemy and would be cut to pieces.

With little choice, I decided they would fight and maybe reduce the enemy's unit strength. Selecting the unit again gave me a formation menu with a little diagram beside each.

*Circle Formation*

*Staggered Formation*

*Square Formation*

The square formation looked to be the most compact and gave them a small defensive boost. Or so I hoped.

*Square Formation selected.*

I watched, helpless, as the footmen unit assembled themselves just as the first of the two grunt units smashed into them.

*Footmen Unit training Complete.*

The new unit assembled outside the barracks.

Now what? I looked around at my base. There were the two footmen units here, one of which split in guard duty, with an archer unit to pop out soon.

Do I send the two footmen units out now and follow up with the archers? Or do I sit here and let my troops die because of my own stupidity?

The abandoned unit was in full engagement now. My combat log started to scroll.

*+1 Battle points*

*+1 Battle points*

*+1 Battle points*

What elation I felt from the damage they were dealing evaporated as I watched their unit icon get smaller and smaller.

It wouldn't take long before they were destroyed. To their north, the other enemy icons kept coming but were generic. No telling what they could be.

Regardless of what they were it spelled trouble for me.

Suppressing my growing panic, I turned my attention to the two base units. I commanded the split unit to forgo their guard duties at the gold mine and the banner alter and reform next to the second unit.

As they moved into position, the third footmen unit finished training and I moved them to stand next to the others.

My gold was now too low to start training another footmen unit which made me more than a little angry.

Keep it together, Vee, I told myself. If I got ticked off every time a messed up, then I'd always be angry.

*Archer Unit training Complete.*

Twelve archers wearing red hooded cloaks appeared next to the range. Each had a short bow and a full quiver of arrows.

The sight of their bows did not give me confidence. They were for limited range which meant they'd be at risk of getting overrun. I would have to keep them to the rear of the footmen units.

*Footmen Unit eliminated.*

I looked to the map with dread.

The footmen icon vanished, and a moment after, all the enemy icons on the map blinked out of existence.

Fog of war. If a unit didn't have line of sight on the enemy, it couldn't be seen on the map.

Now I was blind.

A chat request appeared on my screen. Perplexed, I accepted it.

The scout's smug grin greeted me. "In position, Commander. And I can report multiple enemies located."

Right. I'd forgotten all about this guy. Instead of focusing on all my available assets I was letting the current crisis overwhelm me.

The scout's path had taken him up the east side of the map which linked with the middle area, forming a big circle, just as I suspected. Now he was sitting within the tree line directly east of the center altar.

"Good work," I said. Now I could see what was coming at me. "Let's see what you got."

The scout turned away and the camera view tilted up. Through the trees where he was hiding was the center platform area. The two grunt units that had just killed my footmen could be seen in the distance.

Other enemy units had arrived and were in the process of crossing the river via the altar platform. Two more footmen units and, behind them, two archery units.

Even more appeared in the distance to the north, but I couldn't discern their unit type.

"Can you tell what those are?" I asked, feeling foolish as I squinted at the chat screen.

The scout turned to look at me. "Would you like me to move closer? No problem at all."

"No problem, huh?" I found myself asking. This NPC has got some attitude, and I was intrigued despite myself. "Why is that?"

That crooked grin appeared on his face, again. "Because I'm the best scout you got."

I laughed. "You're the only scout I got!"

"Exactly!" he said, grin widening.

By the Gaming Gods. I thought. Was I actually flirting with this NPC? How stupid was that? Maybe I've been playing this game too long, if that was the case.

Over his shoulder, Amara dropped out of Shadow Form directly behind him. She raised her sword.

"Look out!" I yelled, surprised.

"I am looking out," the scout said with mild confusion. "It's my job to-."

With a swing Amara cut his head off, and just as the chat view terminated I saw her grinning at the camera.

At me.

Now I swore. Curse words flowed like water from a roiling river.

I tried to calm down but only succeeded in making it worse. My hands were shaking with rage.

There was only one thing that could temper my anger.

I pointed at the archer unit. "Fall in behind us and stay close." The archers nodded in unison and moved to stand behind the formation of footmen.

Smoke's respawn timer still had five minutes on it, but that was fine. I'd march with my troops for now.

I ran through the footmen ranks and stood before them. They made quite a sight, albeit a smaller one that I'd like.

"We're heading out to meet the enemy!" I shouted.

All the men cheered, raising their weapons with scattered shouts of, "By Y'Godda!"

I turned and began running northwest, my troops behind me, one unit following the next. My heart was thudding at full speed.

So, Amara wanted a fight? I thought, ticked off.

Fine.

She was going to get one.

# CHAPTER EIGHT

We marched as fast as I could push my army.

Within a few minutes we reached the midway point of the curve but there was no sign of the enemy. Could Amara be camped out at the altar, waiting for me?

My anger had subsided, and I started to think through my plan only to realize I had none. Find Amara and attack. Not very strategic, just a decision based off of emotion.

I looked back at my army. It made for an impressive sight to see them marching along with determined looks. It gave me a bit of a charge.

Thorm, my friend who I'd adventured with many times, went through a long phase where all he played were these Battle Fields. It had become an addiction to the point he even stopped questing in the outer gaming world all together. He attained a championship level and entered competitive ladders. But after a really bad defeat, where he suspected his opponent had cheated but couldn't prove it, he quit Battle Fields all together.

He use to say he loved the charge of leading an army into battle so much he couldn't stop himself from playing.

I'd dismissed that out of hand, until now. There was definitely a unique feeling you got with dozens of troops following you into battle.

Still, I worried these units would be enough. Amara had quite a few assembled before I lost sight of them.

As we marched I'd kept an impatient eye on my gold resource counter. Now it ticked over enough to train a new footmen unit.

"Halt!" I said raising my hand.

In unison, all four units stopped. Staring straight ahead, they quietly waited.

I needed to do some quick micro-managing before continuing on.

First, I put another footmen unit into training. The moment they popped out, I'd have them follow us.

Then I switched the worker unit at the quarry to the gold mine as well. This put all my workers on gold duty. The stone and lumber for buildings and the Keep upgrade could wait. Right now, troops were the priority and gold was desperately needed for them.

Maybe I should use what resources I had to build another barracks? Two units in training were better than one.

I could see how players could spend most of their time just waiting for things to happen. Waiting on resources, waiting on units to train, waiting on units moving.

"Enemy spotted!" shouted one of the footmen in the front unit, and pointed.

Marching quickly toward us from around the northern bend were Amara's units.

Waiting on the enemy was one thing I didn't have to worry about.

"Get ready!" I shouted. My troops tensed.

I surveyed the approaching army.

Two units of troll grunts marched side by side, followed by another grunt unit.

Trailing behind these were two units of troll archers. Even from this distance I saw their bows were the same short variety as my own archers.

As they fully emerged from around the bend, no other units appeared.

I allowed myself a slight sense of relief. Aside from an extra unit of archers, the armies were even. And they had the distinct disadvantage of lacking a commander. Where was Amara?

Turning to my troops I barked out orders, and they reacted quickly.

I brought forward all three of my footmen units and lined them up, side by side. Then, I moved my archer unit in close, but instead of keeping them in a square, I used their formation menu to spread them out in a single line.

The enemy units copied me, bringing their third grunt unit up to step between the other two. Their archer units positioned themselves directly behind the grunts, but did not change their square formations. All this was done without altering their speed.

In moments, they would be at my front lines.

Let them come, I thought with a smile.

*Enemy spotted!*

I blinked in surprise. Where did that come from? Looking past the approaching enemy I didn't see another new unit.

Panicking, I looked behind us. Nothing was there but empty grass.

Then my eyes were drawn to a flashing icon on my map.

The Lookout at the Keep had sent the warning.

He had spotted an enemy unit approaching the base from the northeast. It was an icon I did not immediately recognize. Then cold dread washed over me.

Cavalry!

Amara had *cavalry*? So soon?

My thoughts were cut short as the first elements of the enemy grunts suddenly stepped up their advance as they got closer.

One of the trolls raised his spear and let out a war cry. The other grunts shouted in kind.

I looked to my footmen in confusion. Shouldn't they be shouting, too?

Then all three grunt units slammed into my footmen's front ranks.

Whoa. Things were happening fast. I looked from the fighting troops, with spears and swords flailing, to the icon of the enemy cavalry descending on my defenseless base.

Suddenly, there was the sound of two dozen enemy bows releasing their arrows.

I looked up at the cloud of death from above.

Oh, crap.

The arrows fell into the footmen's ranks where men screamed. But when I looked to my archers, they simply stood with arrows nocked in their bows, doing nothing.

"What are you doing?" I yelled as I ran over to them. "Why aren't you firing back?"

"You want us to fire back?" The archer leader asked.

"Yes!" I shouted, incredulous.

The archers then raised their bows and fired.

"And keep at it," I said. "Don't stop."

"Yes, Commander!" the leader said. They loosed another volley.

What was with that delay?

On a hunch I checked the archer's unit info screen and found an unchecked box at the bottom marked 'Autonomous.'

I checked the box and the archer's leader shouted, "Fire at will!"

If there were time, I would have smacked myself in the head. Under each of the footmen units info screens was the same unchecked box. Cursing to myself, I checked them all.

This had a dramatic effect on the men. Instead of reacting to the trolls attacks, they became aggressive and pushed forward.

Stupid learning curve.

But I didn't have time to lament. On the map, the enemy cavalry icon had cut the distance to my base by half and closed fast. And there were three minutes remaining on the barracks training timer.

Other than a single Lookout, the base was defenseless.

Thankfully, Smoke's respawn timer had ended, and I summoned him. Leaping up into the saddle I shouted to my men who were locked in furious combat. "Hold the line!"

"Yes, Commander!" shouted the different unit leaders, just as another volley of arrows fell into their ranks.

To the archer leader I said, "Concentrate your fire on their archers!"

I looked over the battle.

My footmen were fully entangled with the grunts, swords and spears slashing and jabbing. Both formations were thinning out, but other than the enemy's extra archery unit, the sides appeared even.

I had a sinking feeling it wouldn't be enough.

*Base Under Attack!*

The cavalry icon was now within my base's perimeter and moved up against the Keep.

I had to go. Now.

With frustration, I put my back to my army and charged southward at full speed. The sound of the ferocious battle fading behind me.

When I selected the Keep's icon a health meter appeared.

*Keep: 8,200 / 10,000 hit points.*

As I watched in horror, the 8,200 dropped to 7,900. In no time it would be destroyed which I couldn't let happen.

Never mind holding the banner at the center altar, without the Keep I couldn't create buildings nor hire workers. The game would effectively be over.

Smoke ran like the wind and in less than a minute we rounded the bend. The Keep was in sight.

Mounted trolls hit at the base of the Keep with swords. Smoke started to billow from its arrow slits, and the Lookout valiantly fired his bow down at the attackers.

I took small solace that the cavalry didn't seek out my workers. The worker units were well past the trees, out of view. My gold counter kept steadily rising.

When Smoke got me within range, I readied my bow and fired.

A troll screamed and fell to the ground, his horse racing off.

*+5 Battle Points.*

*You have gained 200 experience points toward your next level.*

But the other riders did not react, only concentrated on smacking away at the Keep's stone base.

*Keep: 5,500 / 10,000 hit points.*

I fired two more times, and both arrows found their mark. This made the remaining attackers change their focus and nine riders turned to face me.

This is going to hurt, I thought, switching to my sword. Then I crashed directly into their ranks.

My first swing sent a head flying away to bounce of the Keep's wall. The next parried a sword thrust by hacking off the owner's arm.

*Parry Skill Increased! Level 6, 21%*

One-on-one these guys were no match for me, but there were too many of them. They used their numbers to crowd me in.

I felt the tip of a blade slice through my cloak and cut deeply into my right shoulder. Another pierced my left thigh.

Smoke took a hit against his flank, and in response kicked back with both legs. I felt it connect, and someone screamed, but I was too busy parrying swords to look.

A rider rammed his own horse into me just as I had stretched out to hit another attacker in the head. My balance was off, and the impact sent me sprawling to the ground.

I found myself suddenly up against the Keep's wall. Troll's and horses crowded around swinging swords and kicking legs.

This is bad, I thought, blocking what I could. Too many of their hits were now connecting. Bad, bad, bad.

*Footmen Unit training complete.*

Through the forest of horse legs I saw the new footmen unit assemble next to the barracks building. They looked over at me expectantly.

"Get your butts over here!" I screamed. A horse had turned in front of me and kicked back. I jumped out of the way as its hoof cracked against the stone wall.

The new footmen unit joined the fray allowing me to recover and mount Smoke. Annoyed beyond reason, I made sure the remaining riders were each decapitated.

Within a minute the cavalry unit was eliminated.

The footmen let out a cheer as I surveyed the damage to the Keep.

*4,800 / 10,000 hit points.*

*Cost to repair: 50 wood & 75 stone & 50 gold per 1,000 hit points.*

Wonderful, I thought glumly. Repairing this would cause further delay in, well, everything else.

As I caught my breath, I assigned one of the worker units from the gold mine to begin repairs on the Keep. They appeared through the trees and smacked the outside of the Keep with hammers.

It was like watching the cavalry unit attack, but in reverse. The Keep's hit points began to slowly climb up.

"Commander, what should we do with these?" asked a footman. He held one of the cavalry horses by the bridle. I looked around and saw at least eight or nine more of the animals wandering about.

"Can you ride them?" I asked.

"Yes," the footman said. "If you are willing to pay for the training." A tile appeared next to the man's head.

*Upgrade this footmen unit to cavalry unit.*

*Cost 200 gold. Yes/No?*

My gold counter was at zero and the moment any was added it vanished. I realized that the repair work to the Keep was taking it all.

I selected No.

"Going to have to wait on the upgrade for a little while guys," I told the footman. "Until then, corral these horses together and place them in the barracks."

The footman saluted and the men set about capturing the horses.

Well, at least I'd get a cavalry unit out of this mess, I thought.

Then I noticed a message appear in my combat log, with a bunch of previous ones I hadn't noticed in the heat of battle.

*Footmen Unit Eliminated.*

Oh, shoot. I looked to my map just in time to see the last unit icon of my forces fighting on the plains blink out.

All three footmen units and the lone archer unit were no longer present on the map.

My army had been destroyed.

I cursed. Could this situation possible get any worse?

*You Banner Has Been Taken!*

What?!

My head snapped around to the altar.

There, clutching the red banner in her hands was Amara. She must have snuck in under Shadow Form during the fighting.

Before I could react, she summoned her mount and jumped into the saddle with a single leap. Then she charged off.

"Eat FILTERED, ya FILTERED!" She screamed.

By the Gaming Gods.

Amara had my banner!

# CHAPTER NINE

Recovering from my shock, I leapt onto Smoke and gave chase.

Amara's white horse was frighteningly fast, and I hoped Smoke could catch up with it. She headed to the northeast curve of the lower circle. I figured she didn't want to risk running into any potential elements of my now defeated army on the western curve.

Regardless, her destination was clear: The central platform. There, once the banner was placed and held for five minutes, she would win.

Grass blurred underneath me, and trees whipped by. My eyes were locked onto her back. Although out of range for the moment, I switched to my bow and summoned a magma arrow. If it killed her before, it could do it again.

I should have suspected the cavalry attack was meant to cause a distraction while she got close to the banner in Shadow Form.

Had I kept a footman unit on the altar, this probably wouldn't have happened. But, admittedly, I was having a difficult time managing everything that was going on.

My newbie-ness to the Battle Field would now cost me the Lost War Banner of Y'godda, and beyond that, mess up my chance at returning it for the quest reward.

I hated failing at quests. Sure, it happened once in a while. But this time I'd fail because another player took it from me.

Anger blossomed in my chest, and I kicked at Smoke unnecessarily to close the gap.

As our chase rounded the curve, an enemy unit appeared. Grunts. Then, behind them, a unit of archers.

Amara was racing directly toward them.

I didn't have much time, so I nocked the magma arrow. The speed we were travelling coupled with Smoke's galloping motion messed with my aim, but I only had one chance to take her out.

I fired.

The arrow flew right at her. But, instead of striking her in the back and giving me the glorious show of watching her bubble away into a puddle of lava, the arrow zinged past her head.

Quickly, I summoned a full quiver of normal arrows and shot at her. It would be awhile before I could use another magma arrow, with a twenty minute cooldown.

One struck her steed in the rump, but the rest missed completely.

Ahead, the troll grunts broke from their square formation and spread out into a single line, spears at the ready.

I already knew I wouldn't catch up with her but that didn't cause me to slow down. She had the banner.

The grunts made a space in the middle of their protective line, and Amara charged through it. Then the archers fired a volley.

This made me pull up short, yanking hard on Smoke's reins. As I tried to turn us away, I knew I'd screwed up again.

Arrows fell around me. One pierced my thigh, and two others struck Smoke's side.

Smoke reared in pain, and I desperately tried to keep control of him.

The archers brought out new arrows. Behind them was the retreating form of Amara, my red banner flapping wildly in the wind.

The grunts moved forward at a run and the archers fired, again.

"Go!" I shouted. Poor Smoke nickered and bucked and I thought I'd be thrown to the ground.

Thankfully, he let me turn him south and he bolted into a full run.

Arrows thudded around us.

After we had run several hundred paces, I stopped and looked back.

Amara's distant form vanished around the bend, and with it, my hope of catching her.

What could I do? Soon she would be at the platform.

My mind raced.

There was only one thing I could do, even if the outcome would be the same.

I kicked Smoke into a run. As we headed south, I looked at my poor beleaguered base on the map.

My one footman unit stood near the Keep. Then I remembered the horses. The cavalry upgrade.

But my gold was near zero. The repairs to the Keep were still ongoing and sucking up what gold was being actively mined.

With frustration growing, I pulled the worker unit off the Keep and sent them back to the gold mine.

The gold level started to rise, but not fast enough for my liking.

We reached the base, but I continued on past it toward the western curve. The footmen waved. There was no time to do anything here. Not even to stop and heal in the Keep.

I sent a command to the footmen's leader to upgrade to cavalry once 200 gold had been collected. Then, he was to take his unit directly to the central platform via the western curve.

In my heart I knew it would not be enough, but since the game was close to ending, I felt like I needed to at least try.

If I was going to fail, I'd fail while using everything available to me.

The base passed from view as I rounded the western bend and headed north. I saw past the trees the beam of light in the sky which indicated the location of my banner.

Had she reached the platform?

*Red Banner Placed. Five minute countdown begins.*

Yup.

A timer appeared at the top right of my vision and started counting down.

As I continued north, I passed the location of the battle. There were no bodies or discarded weapons as the game cleaned them up after a short time.

I almost expected to run into any remaining elements of the troll units, but it appeared whoever survived had been pulled back.

Approaching the final bend that lead to the middle section and the platform, I felt my heart sink. I'd really messed this whole thing up, right from the beginning.

Having avoided playing on Battle Fields all these years was now going to cost me. At that moment, I resolved to actively try them after this. If my future questing even had a slight chance of ending up on a Battle Field, I wanted to be ready.

But first, I had to suffer the agony of defeat.

A sudden break in the trees to the east made me pull Smoke to a stop who nickered in protest.

It was the path through the forest. The one that lead to Grax.

I looked at my Battle Points counter. 1,200. The exact amount required to hire him into my service.

A smile spread across my face.

Leaving Smoke at the edge of the trees, I ran through the forest along the path, my heart pounding with excitement.

When I arrived at the little clearing, Grax was waiting expectantly.

"You are here to free me?" the ogre rumbled.

"I free you, and you help me, agreed?" I asked.

He regarded me for several long, agonizing moments, then nodded his huge head. "If you can afford the price, I am yours to command."

Inwardly, I sighed with relief. When I pulled up his information screen it asked if I wished to hire this champion for 1,200 Battle points.

"Heck, yeah!" I said and selected Yes.

*Champion Unit hired.*

My Battle points counter dropped to zero. The manacles around Grax's wrists unlocked and fell heavily to the ground.

The ogre grinned and slowly stood. By the Gaming Gods, he was huge! Easily two stories tall and nearly as wide as my Keep.

Grax stretched his thick arms which resembled massive oaks. "It will be good to fight again. Who shall I crush for you first?"

*Four Minute Warning!*

"Funny you should ask that," I said. "Let's get to the central platform, quickly."

"And then?" he asked.

"Crush everything there."

The ogre's grin grew wider. "That is a good plan, Commander."

We moved down the pathway, Grax's colossal frame bumping into trees, snapping them or felling them over.

Emerging from the tree line, I was startled to see my new cavalry unit running toward me.

The unit leader raised a hand in greeting, but I pointed northward.

"To the platform!" I shouted. He nodded and thundered past.

As I leapt onto Smoke, Grax practically exploded out of the forest, sending branches and trees flying everywhere. In his hands was a large log, a makeshift club. Placing one end on his shoulder, he turned and ran north, heavy footfalls shaking the ground.

Wow, I thought, kicking Smoke into a gallop to catch up with the sprinting ogre. The champion's size and speed was terrifying. I was just thankful he was on my side.

We rushed northward, and I made sure that the cavalry did not get too far ahead. As fast as Grax was, he wasn't faster than a horse at full charge.

With no clue what we were about to face, we rounded the final bend. The anticipation was high.

The grassy plains widened and the river with the platform came into view.

Enemy units were assembled there.

Two grunt units stood side by side on the southern edge of the platform, in square formation. They practically bristled with spears.

On the north side of the platform were two units of archers spread out in a double line.

And at the altar on the platform was my red banner, clutched by a skeletal hand. Beside it, sitting on her horse, was Amara.

Oh, boy, I thought taking in the army before me. Could this get any worse?

*Enemy Spotted!*

Confused, I looked to my map.

The Lookout at the Keep had spotted enemy units incoming from the northeast. It was the grunts and archers which had stopped me from chasing Amara. Now they were marching on my base.

With a quick check at my gold levels I assigned both a footmen unit and archer unit to training. Hopefully, they would pop out in time to save the base.

*Three Minute Warning!*

And speaking of time.

All three of us, me, Grax, and my lone cavalry unit, continued our suicidal charge at the platform. There was nothing else I could do.

Ownership of the banner would be decided in the next few moments. All or nothing, here we go.

As we closed the distance to the waiting grunt units, I pointed my sword forward and screamed the one word which would now decide me fate.

"Attack!"

# CHAPTER TEN

A horrific volley of arrows rained upon us, but did not affect our speed. I did not have time to check everyone's damage, but neither I nor Smoke were hit.

Just short of the bristling spear line, I stopped, letting Grax and the cavalry charge past. Switching to my bow I fired wildly into the assembled grunts. No point getting speared to death before the fight even started. Let the heavy units take them on.

And take them on, they did.

The cavalry charged headlong into the first grunt unit, horses stomping over bodies, spears snapping with the impact. The riders were screaming with rage and swinging their swords.

Grax ran straight into the other unit of grunts. But before he got within spear range, he heaved his log with both hands over one shoulder and swung it across like a bat in a wide arc.

Grunts and spears flew everywhere. One grunt even pinwheeled over the platform to bounce into the archers.

Figuring Grax had the advantage for the moment, I concentrated my arrow fire on the grunts engaged with the cavalry.

I risked a glance at Amara. Bow in hand, she hadn't moved, nor made any indication she was going to join in just yet. Plastered across her face was a smug smile.

She knew she had this.

Getting angry, I aimed my bow in her direction. But the archers fired again.

Since they couldn't aim at the enemy tangling with their own units, they settled on the easier target.

Me.

The sky darkened with a swarm of descending arrows.

Crap! I yanked on Smoke's reins and moved us out of the way just in time.

Two dozen arrows sprouted from the ground I'd just vacated.

In response, I fired back at the archers, hitting three in quick succession. But it wouldn't be enough. If left alone, those archers would eventually kill us all.

*Archery Skill Increased! Level 8, 82%*

Taking a tremendous risk, I shouted a command at the cavalry leader.

"Ignore the grunts! Kill the archers!"

The cavalry leader reacted instantly. His riders immediately disengaged from the grunts, and trampling over some of them, charged across the platform.

Before the grunts could turn to follow, I took Smoke into their ranks, switching to my sword and swinging like a lunatic.

To my right, Grax was stomping on grunts with his huge feet, and batting others into the air with log swings. But the survivors kept fighting, jabbing with their spears into his legs.

Focusing on my own fight, I smacked away spear thrusts while using Smoke's size to push through the grunts. One decapitation followed another.

At the periphery, my cavalry unit, already severally depleted having started short several men, was slaughtering one of the archer units, who had now routed.

The other archer unit fired at my cavalry with impunity while keeping their distance.

I cursed myself for not telling the cavalry to split themselves across both archer units. Now one archer unit served as bait while the other worked on finishing their attackers off.

But I had no time to deal with this screw up. Smoke took a hard hit with a spear into his rear left leg and stumbled. The horse had received too much damage previously, and racing headlong into this fight without time to heal had taken its toll.

Smoke teetered over to his right side, then collapsed. Feeling this about to occur, I barely leapt from the saddle over probing spear blades, and tumbled to the ground.

*Your Mount has been slain.*

Up on my feet again, Grax's shadow passed over me. He'd crushed and stomped the entire grunt unit on his own.

"More battle," he said as he strode into the remaining grunts. "More blood."

"All yours!" I said, relieved. A glance at Amara showed her still rooted in the same spot, only this time with a sword, but the same smug look on her face. What was she doing? She could have at least assisted her men with her bow and not given up her defense of the altar.

Confused, I was about to run over to her when I noticed the last two riders of my cavalry cut down the final archer.

But there was still the other archer unit. They fired a volley and one of the riders went down. The lone rider still charged at them. I knew he wouldn't make it.

And once he was dead, those archers could easily take me out with a single volley.

*Two Minute Warning!*

I gave Amara a nasty look. She just smiled at me from her mount, unmoving.

Convinced she wouldn't attack, at least for the moment, I shouted to Grax. "Go crush those archers!"

Grax immediately turned and raced toward them, causing a grunt to bounce of his leg and go flying. The remaining grunts tried to follow him but he was too fast.

The last rider fell to the archer's volley, but not before Grax stomped into them, log-club swinging.

I turned to Amara, sword at the ready. "You and I have some unfinished business."

She stared at me from atop her mount, grinning like an idiot.

Not waiting for a reply, I ran at her, then jumped. I sailed through the air, screaming like a banshee. Just before the moment of impact, I swung my sword.

And I sailed straight through her and tumbled across the platform.

I spun around and looked at her in confusion. She wasn't solid. Phased?

Sensing a trap, I cautiously moved closer to her, and swung my sword at the front legs of her horse.

The sword passed through them, like they were nothing but air.

Annoyed, and even more confused by now, I walked forward into the ghostly image swinging my sword.

Amara and her horse suddenly flickered then vanished.

It was a trick. It wasn't Amara at all. She'd left this image of her as a decoy. Where was she?

Then it hit me. If she wasn't here, then my banner was unguarded.

I moved toward the altar to take the banner from the outstretched hand of the skeletal altar.

Four remaining grunts suddenly rushed in to block my way, forming a line with spears at the ready.

I snorted a laugh. This wouldn't take much. A glance at Grax showed he had crushed the archer's unit down to five men. The banner was as good as mine.

A quick swing took out the closest grunt. But as I stepped in to take out the rest, I noticed movement in the trees to the north of the platform.

A rider, wearing mostly gray with a blue vest, emerged from the forest and I recognized it as Amara. Behind her, from within the thick forest, something huge moved. An orange light appeared there and grew brighter.

Suddenly, a tall being stepped out into the clearing. It was a tree, in the shape of a man, with arms and legs. I'd seen similar before in my questing life and knew it to be a Treant. But this was much bigger than any I'd encountered before.

A champion.

And being a champion, it couldn't be any old run of the mill Treant. It was on fire. Where there should have been leaves, there were large orange flames. Huge fires burned at the ends of its arms. Large cracks in its trunk formed a kind of face, with eyes and a mouth. And from within those, a fire burned.

Shocked, I took in these new arrivals. This was not good.

The Fire Treant ran forward toward Grax.

Amara kicked at her horse and galloped toward the platform, racing past Grax who was busy crushing the head of an archer with a hand.

Grax finally noticed the giant flaming tree coming at him. He turned to meet the attack, swinging his log-club.

The Fire Treant raised a flaming hand and grabbed the log-club, stopping the mighty swing. It plunged its other flaming hand into Grax's face.

Grax bellowed in agony.

*One Minute Warning!*

Uh-oh. Things were getting out of hand quickly.

With Amara racing toward the platform, I attacked the grunts blocking my way to the banner. Two sword swipes left two of them dead. The last held his ground.

Amara reached the platform and galloped toward me.

I feinted in one direction, causing the last grunt to stab at empty air. Then I sliced his head off.

With no time left, I didn't even bother to look at Amara. Instead, I leapt at the altar and grabbed the banner by its long wooden handle.

The skeletal hand released its grip. The banner was mine!

*You have retrieved your banner!*

Amara slammed into me with her mount sending me sprawling to the ground. The banner popped out of my grasp and skidded across the platform where it stopped, standing straight up like a flag pole.

*Your banner has been dropped!*

I'd had it! I touched it! Why didn't it get returned?

But Amara would not give me pause to think through this annoying new conundrum. She dropped from her horse and attacked me with her sword.

I got to my feet just in time to parry her swings, which were fast and savage. Her face was scrunched with rage.

"You FILTERED FILTERED!" she screamed swinging at me.

So fierce was her attack, I couldn't even counter with my own. It took everything I had to parry her swings.

"You need a more original vocabulary," I said between her strikes. A glance told me where the banner was. But why hadn't it returned? Was I suppose to do something?

*Thirty Second Warning!*

She angled herself between me and the banner. I had the frightening realization she was at full health, and my own was now less than twenty percent. Arrows and spears had taken their toll.

"This whole thing should have been finished at the start," she said and launched into a quick succession of attacks.

She pushed me back so fast, I had to somersault backward over the altar.

*Acrobatics Skill Increased! Level 3, 56%*

Landing on the other side, I asked, "What the heck do you want with my quest item? It's mine! I worked for it, not you."

Amara marched around the altar but I moved the other way. For several moments she chased me in circles.

I wanted to laugh, or would have if the game wasn't about to end.

*Twenty Second Warning!*

"The banner is worth a fortune on the auction house," Amara said, trying to catch me. "It's worth more to me than to you, FILTERED."

Beyond her I could see Grax and the Fire Treant locked in each other's grasp. Fire danced over Grax's body. Even the arrows sticking out of his back were on fire. Both were bellowing at each other with deafening roars.

"When I win this," I said, "I'll buy you a dictionary."

Suddenly, Grax dropped his flaming log-club and, while holding the Fire Treant close with the other hand, drove his fist into the Treant's mouth.

"You're just going to buy your way to the nearest crypt in a second. This game is mine!" Amara said, trying to get close. She was unaware of what was happening with her champion.

Grax yanked something out of the Treant's mouth that looked like a wooden heart. The Tree champion's flames intensified, then sputtered, and went out.

*Ten Second Warning!*

"Doesn't look good for your friend," I said with a nod over her shoulder.

Amara blinked in momentary confusion and, as she turned impulsively to look, I made a break for the banner.

Amara screamed and chased after me. As I passed her, she struck out and sliced my right leg.

A warning on my screen told me that leg was now useless. I sprawled to the ground but my momentum took me within reach of the banner.

I grabbed it with my free hand.

*You have retrieved your banner!*

*Five Second Warning!*

Amara descended on me, bringing her sword down with a heavy swing.

From the ground, I barely deflected the blow. The tip of her blade sliced my abdomen.

*Four Seconds!*

I tried to scramble to my feet, but another swing from Amara kept me down as I blocked it. She was screaming like a maniac.

*Three Seconds!*

Then I realized what I needed to do. The banner didn't just need to be removed from the altar. It had to be taken off the platform, too!

Abandoning my own defense, I clutched the banner close to me with one hand and, dismissing my sword, used the other to crawl/fall backward to the edge of the platform which was only a few paces away.

Amara stayed close and slashed my left thigh.

*Two Seconds!*

My health was now at five percent and one leg refused to cooperate. Still, I managed to twist my body around and throw myself toward the platform's edge.

*One Second!*

With both arms outstretched, I slid along the platform on my side like sliding into home plate. The bottom end of the banner's wooden handle slipped over the very edge of the platform to touch the dirt outside it.

The banner vanished.

*Your banner has been returned to base!*

But I didn't have time to process this, let alone celebrate. I looked up as Amara loomed over me.

I saw the briefest image: Amara bringing her sword down upon me, eyes wild with rage. And towering behind Amara was Grax, the ogre's clothes and hair aflame. He, too, was swinging his flaming log-club downward, but at Amara's head.

Then my view-screen went black, and a message appeared.

*You have been slain in battle!*

# CHAPTER ELEVEN

My heart was racing and sweat cloyed at my skin beneath my simulation suit.

I felt jubilation at recovering my banner having no clue what had been required to do so. This only strengthened my resolve to play Battle Fields more often and perhaps study guides on military strategy.

Now I can see why Thorm became so addicted to them. Those last few moments fighting at the platform were some of the most intense I'd experienced playing this game in years. There were previous tough encounters, but not quite like that.

And I hoped there would be many more.

My thoughts went to Amara. She'd used that flaky hologram trick as a weak ploy to buy her time while she fetched the Flame Treant champion. And it worked, too.

Was Grax okay? Before dying, I didn't get the chance to see if more enemy units were racing toward the platform. As far as I knew, he was the only one left standing after all that fighting.

But as the blackness of my screen brightened to reveal me laying in the crypt, my attention shifted from my wounded champion to my wounded Keep.

The map revealed that the enemy troll grunts, backed by archers, had attacked the base. The Keep was damaged to just under half its hit points.

Thankfully, both the footmen and archers I set to training had emerged to stop the assault.

Now, both forces were entangled in a ferocious fight. Even down in the crypt I could hear the clashing of weapons and screams of the dying.

*Amara Frostwalker has been reborn to the world. Let the Battle continue!*

I felt a little sense of victory knowing Amara had been squashed like a bug by Grax. But when I looked at my combat log, I'd only received 100 Battle Points for her death, while she got 1,000 for mine.

It had to be because I wasn't the one who killed her. Whatever. I'll take it for now and hope to come across another champion to spend it on.

I leapt from the slab and raced up the stairs. Emerging from the floor of the Keep revealed the damage which had already been done. Huge cracks webbed the walls and black smoke filled the upper ceiling.

But even through this I saw the Lookout wave down at me, then disappear.

Not wasting another moment, I raced outside.

Troll grunts lunged at footmen who parried and countered. My human archers had taken up position to one side of the archery range and fired volleys at the troll archers standing a short distance to the north.

I judged the strength of both forces to be about even. But now I joined the fray.

Striking out at the nearest troll, I dodged a spear jab by rolling to the ground. Standing, I thrust my sword up through the jaw of another troll.

A flashing icon on the map drew my eyes. It was Grax asking for new orders.

What was I doing? Other things needed my immediate attention right now. Fighting would come second. My men could handle this for a few more moments.

I ran through the fight to stand in the doorway of the Keep, mindful of arrant arrows and spears.

Grax appeared severely injured, but alive.

"I need more trolls to crush," he told me from the chat view. His hair and eyebrows were all gone, burnt away. Wisps of smoke curled up from his blackened flesh.

With a laugh, I said, "Don't worry, there will be more trolls. I promise."

He peered about, somewhat disappointed. "Now what shall I do?"

Good question. Bringing him south to the base would be helpful. He could help guard while I repaired the buildings and built up another army.

But that would leave the platform undefended. Right now, with Grax there, it was in my control. Even if Amara managed to sneak down here and snatch the banner away again, she'd have a burnt, angry Grax to contend with when she reached the middle.

Also, without a scout or other unit in the vicinity, Grax could see what was coming from the north. And maybe keep them from moving further south just by his presence.

It wouldn't last long. He was injured and alone now. But as a temporary stopgap it'd have to do.

"Guard the platform. If a solo unit is dumb enough to try to cross it take them out. But if there is more than you can handle, fall back, and come to the base."

Grax frowned. "I can handle all units. No problem. I hope I don't have to wait too long."

I hoped we got to wait a long time and closed the chat. Time was needed now to get things in order.

The sound of the surrounding battle brought my thoughts back to the immediate situation. I went into the command menu and put another footmen and archer unit into training. Thankfully, my workers had been diligently mining away this entire time so gold was not an issue. But it soon would be.

With a final check of the map, I then launched into the fray, sword swinging.

In less than a minute, I helped my footmen eliminate the last of the grunts. Then we ran at the archers who managed a single volley before my forces cut into them.

One archer managed to hit me in the thigh which only ticked me off. More sword swings (and a little swearing) and the archers were decimated.

I looked around. The remaining men of my two units raised their weapons in a cheer.

"Yay for us," I said, but didn't feel it. There was too much to do. Right now, Amara was frantically building up an army, and I had little doubt she would make it sizable before marching south.

I assigned the footman to the banner altar. They would not move from there ever again if I had anything to say about it.

The archers, I sent north along the western curve to link up with Grax. I ordered the unit leader to assemble in a double line formation on the south edge of the platform. That way, they could support Grax when he engaged any approaching units.

It wasn't much but still better than nothing.

Then I turned my attention to my poor beleaguered Keep, which billowed smoke from every opening.

*Keep: 2,200 / 10,000 hit points.*

Those enemy units had really done a number on it, but thankfully they didn't succeed in razing it to the ground.

For this, I pulled one unit of workers off mining duty and assigned them to Keep repairs. It would be very expensive and repairing it fully would take too long and take up too many resources. So I resolved to bring it up to 5,000 hit points, at least.

With the workers on repairs I looked around. Other than waiting for units to finish training, and gold to be mined, there wasn't much else I could do but wait.

So I did.

Once the footmen and archer units emerged I sent them both north together with orders to guard the platform.

While I controlled the middle, I didn't have to worry about enemy units suddenly appearing at the base.

Another archer unit went into training, but instead of another footmen unit I chose a scout next, on a whim.

When he popped out, I sent him north along the east curve (just in case an rogue enemy unit was sitting there) with orders to move past the middle section and scout the enemy base, if possible.

At this point, the Keep repairs reached halfway. But instead of sending these workers back to the mine, I sent them to the neglected quarry.

My intention was to upgrade the Keep, and for that I'd need a lot more stone. Once upgraded, I'd have more worker units, and thus more resources quicker.

Unless Amara screwed things up for me, again.

*Enemy Spotted!*

My heart leapt in my chest. The map showed an enemy cavalry unit approaching the platform from the northeast.

Grax was already moving to intercept them.

The lone archer unit I sent earlier was now just arriving at the platform and formed a double line along its southern edge.

Freaking out a little, I commanded Grax to fall back to the platform. From there, he'd have the support of the archers. Running headlong into the cavalry in his injured state would be the end of him.

Grax grumbled in protest but did as commanded. The cavalry unit drew close but stopped just past the range of the archers.

I could sense Grax's anticipation. He really wanted to kill someone. But he needed to wait.

We'd all have a chance to die soon enough.

The cavalry unit then turned and casually trotted back to the northeast and vanished around the bend. I thought this was a little strange. Without a unit in plain view, Amara wouldn't be able to see the central area. Which meant she must have placed a scout nearby.

I was also convinced that the cavalry unit had meant to draw Grax away.

Soon the footman and archer unit arrived at the middle, much to my relief. I split the archer unit in two and had each half line up on either side of the platform along the river's edge.

Then I set the footmen directly on the platform with orders not to move. They weren't there to protect the altar, since Amara would need the banner first for it to be of any danger, but to block anyone from trying to cross. I didn't think the river could by forded, at least not without a lot of difficulty so the platform was doubly important to control.

The next pair of archers and footmen were sent north, too. I felt confident that the only potential attack on the base now would be a solo Amara and could be dealt with. So any more units I trained were to be sent north immediately.

But not now. Instead, of building up my forces, I decided to wait and upgrade the Keep. I already had enough lumber, it was gold and stone that needed to accumulate.

This seemed to take ages, but the rate of gathering was pretty much even. By the time I had enough of everything the last two units I'd sent north were in position.

I then highlighted the Keep and purchased the upgrade option.

The tower Keep morphed instantly into a wider version of itself. The walls became thicker and more arrows slots appeared. Not much different.

Then I noticed not one but six Lookouts waving down at me, each armed with a crossbow. The defensive radius also expanded and easily enveloped the banner's altar.

Nice. I pulled up the command menu and saw the option to hire more workers. Three of ten units currently active.

Sweet! Seven more worker units, here we come!

One hundred gold produced a new unit that stumbled out of the Keep's door. I sent them to the gold mine. Now I just had to wait for the gold to accumulate and I'd hire the other six.

Things were looking up.

*Enemy Spotted!*

My eyes flew to the map.

At the middle, enemy units were approaching from both northern directions. And there were a lot of them.

Four units from the northwest curve, and another four from the northeast. And that was just what my own units could see.

Amara was coming now, and it looked like she intended on seizing the platform back.

I found myself smiling.

Time for war.

# CHAPTER TWELVE

I glanced over my unit icons at the middle.

Archers were positioned on the southern side of the platform and along the river. The footmen units were placed side by side on the northern edge with one standing directly on the platform. I also placed Grax next to the altar.

For now, this was as defensive as I could get. Once battle was engaged, I could rely on their strategic positioning to hold the line and, hopefully, repel any attack.

Or so I told myself. How the heck would I even know this would work having never even played the most basic of strategy games beyond chess?

Anyways, with the middle firmly locked for the moment I returned my attention to my base.

With the gold now accumulating faster, I hired another two more worker units and set one each to the woodyard and the gold mine.

The next worker unit I set to building a cavalry grounds which I positioned next to the archery range.

While I waited for them to build it up, I kept a tense eye on the middle.

Amara had moved her armies close but stopped both about twenty paces away from my archer's maximum range. Both sets had two footmen at the front with two archer units at the back.

I didn't think she'd attack with these units, yet. She'd wait until reinforcements arrived then hit with overwhelming force.

If I attacked her now, it would only serve to drain my own strength. Had I cavalry up there, then I'd use them to attack immediately, followed up with footmen and archers. This would also allow Grax to become the wandering agent of carnage he craved to be.

But I needed to wait. No doubt Amara was doing similar right now, building up her cavalry, the strongest unit available to us outside of champions.

*Cavalry Grounds complete.*

A long set of stalls were erected next to a wide field with a small obstacle course.

From the command menu I selected the cavalry unit.

*Unit: Cavalry*

*Race: Human*

*Hit Points: 120*

*Speed: 35*

*Weapon: Sword*

*Cost: 500 gold*

When my gold counter hit that number, I selected to train my first official cavalry unit.

*Training time: 7 minutes.*

Horses appeared within the stalls, and a rider with a mount ran through the grounds, jumping over obstacles.

Ouch. With their expensive cost and longer training time, it would take awhile to amass a sizable group of them.

With another glance to ensure nothing had changed at the middle, I hired the remainder of my worker units. I reassigned all units of workers to the gold mine, but kept two on lumber duties and one on the quarry.

With the Keep upgraded, I'd now concentrate on training units as fast as possible. The plan was to build another cavalry ground and maybe second barracks, to help with output.

Suddenly, I got a report from the scout, whom I'd completely forgotten about. He was positioned about half way up the northeast approach to Amara's base, hidden in the trees. He'd snuck past all the enemy units assembled at the middle undetected.

"Incoming cavalry," he said. From his view point I could see two units of trolls on horseback trotting south.

"Okay," I said, feeling what optimism I had deflated a little. "Keep heading north and give me a view of Amara's base."

"Yes, commander," the scout said and signed off. This guy wasn't as cocky as the previous one which made conversation a little more robotic.

There was nothing I could do right now about those cavalry units. I knew they'd be coming, and more would follow.

As I impatiently waited for my own cavalry to finish, I selected another footmen and archer unit to train as the money became available.

The gold was pouring in, for which I was immensely grateful.

By now the enemy cavalry had arrived at the middle and placed themselves to one side of the main force on the northeast approach.

Then from the northwest approach, two other cavalry units appeared.

Okay, things were about to get real, and I'd be more help at the middle than here. Quickly, I assigned two worker units to build another cavalry grounds, which sped up its construction.

As this finished being built the new cavalry unit appeared and formed up next to the stalls. I promptly sent them to the middle at full speed, ensuring they were set to autonomous.

I started training another.

At the middle, the two new enemy cavalry units positioned themselves similarly to the northwest formation. Things were getting cramped up there. Only a matter of time until something snapped.

The second cavalry grounds finished, and I assigned the workers to another barracks. This would be it in terms of buildings for now. I'd considered trying to build barracks closer to the middle, but I just didn't have time, yet. If I survived the impending battle in the middle, a base near the platform could be considered.

Another archer and footmen unit popped out, and north they went.

As I trained more, I dug into the command menu a little. Surely there was a way to get all this automated, so I didn't need to keep watching training timers.

Then I found an option to set up a training queue that encompassed all my training buildings, not just individually. Thank the Gaming Gods. No doubt, Amara had been using this since the beginning which helped train units more efficiently, without waiting on a commander to initiate things.

Trying not to get too annoyed with my noob status, I set up a queue that prioritized cavalry training, followed by footmen, then archers. As the required resources became available, the next unit in the queue would be trained. Each unit would then move quickly to the middle area.

Now I placed all ten of my worker units at the gold mine. Without needing to construct more buildings or upgrade the keep, the need for stone was nil. And I had more than enough wood stockpiled for now.

It was all about the gold, and how fast I could get it.

With that taken care of, my attention could be moved to leading an army, rather than building one.

As if on cue, enemy units started to move. All four cavalry units were withdrawing and moving back northwards.

What the heck? There was nowhere else to go but back to their base, and the middle was where the fight was going to be.

Regardless, I had to get up there. With a final look around my base to ensure the lone footman and archer units still guarded my banner's altar, I summoned Smoke and headed out.

Speeding north, my attention remained glued to the map.

Now all four enemy cavalry units stopped a short distance from the rear of the formations. The two to the northwest then turned around, facing southward, one lined up behind the other. The cavalry units in the northeast did the same.

As I passed the halfway point to the middle, four more enemy cavalry units appeared. Two for each approach. These lined up behind the others.

Now there were two lines of four cavalry units all facing the middle.

This could not be good.

Coming around the final bend to the middle, I passed several of my own units, en route. But I didn't give them any mind, so focused on the strange behavior of the enemy cavalry.

What was Amara up to? And was she commanding her units from her base? Her icon was nowhere on the map and my scout in the northeast was not in any position yet to see her.

I arrived at the platform, a little relieved that nothing else had changed since the strange enemy movements. My gut instinct told me I needed to do something with my formation now while I still had a chance.

Whether this would be a mistake or not, only time would tell.

Quickly, I moved my units forward. By splitting them in two, one group to face each enemy formation, I hoped to counter being hit by one massive army.

I set my footmen in the front, three units side by side, followed by archers and cavalry to the northwest. A similar group went northeast.

The idea was not to engage the enemy, but block them from joining up with the other group.

Thankfully, (or maybe worriedly) none of the enemy units reacted to this sudden shift of my forces. Either Amara wasn't paying attention, or she was laughing at my folly.

Regardless, in less than a minute I now had both approaches blocked with footmen units spread out from the river all the way to the trees to the north.

In the small space between these blocking formations I placed most of my remaining units. I still had more coming from the base, and a grumbling Grax standing next to the altar.

Not quite certain what to do at this point, I let Amara make the next move.

She did not disappoint.

As one, both enemy formations suddenly moved. But instead of forward, they shifted to the sides, forming a large gap down their middle. At the back end of this gap was the first unit of each cavalry line.

Uh-oh, I thought.

The cavalry from both approaches launched into a charge and moved as a line down the gap between units, straight at my waiting defensive wall of footmen.

I reacted the only way I could, by ordering all archer units to fire at will.

By the time they let loose their volley, the first enemy cavalry unit had already raced past their forward line, and into the space which separated the armies.

Arrows found their marks, sending trolls and horses spilling to the ground. But this did not blunt their charge one iota.

On both sides, the cavalry slammed into my waiting footmen units. As each cavalry unit emerged from their army's gap, they altered their trajectory slightly to pass the engaged cavalry to slam into the next unit of footmen.

It took less than tens seconds for all this to transpire, and now each enemy cavalry unit was stomping and fighting their way through my forward lines.

The footmen to the northwest started to buckle under the assault.

Enemy archers moved forward and began firing volley's in the rear of the footmen's formations.

In turn, my own archers fired back and soon the sky was filled with zinging clouds of arrows flying back and forth.

I looked from the frontlines to my assembled forces around the platform. There were so many now, they practically filled the space south of the platform down to the trees. More were arriving every few minutes and even started to form a line from either approach.

As both sides took losses, they would be replaced. Back and forth it would go, for how long was anyone's guess. Maybe Amara would finally gain control of the platform, but I'd fight to get it back.

This entire situation was one big meat grinder, and Amara and I were simply feeding into it.

I shook my head. With so many units at our disposal and the gold flowing continuously, this fight could go on forever.

Something was needed to tip the balance.

Suddenly, there was a deafening shriek from above.

I looked up, shielding my eyes from the sunlight.

High above was a bird, flying from the north over the trees. And it wasn't any old bird, it was huge.

Atop the bird sat a rider, and her gray garb with blue highlights made her identifiable even from such a height.

Amara.

She was coming to attack the platform.

I pulled up the giant bird's stats.

*Name: Yuinnick*

*Race: Great Eagle*

*Rank: Champion*

*Hit Points: 500*

*Speed: 60 (flight)*

*Y'godda's Aerial mount.*

This was not good. Amara had used the Battle points she gained from killing me to hire that thing.

Why can't I have a dang aerial mount?

Getting over my initial surprise, I shouted orders for the units at the platform to tighten up and for the archers to be ready.

If Amara wanted to make a suicidal run at the platform, I'd be happy to oblige her.

But instead of descending, the bird kept flying, its massive shadow passing over me.

As it kept going, a cold realization grabbed me.

She wasn't coming to the platform at all. She was flying south.

To my banner.

# CHAPTER THIRTEEN

Oh, crap.

For several moments, I simply gaped at Amara and her new champion mount as they sailed out of view over the southern trees.

Had I known a flying champion mount was on the Battlefield I would have made a point of locating it. And if I couldn't hire it, I'd set a guard to keep it from Amara.

But there was no point lamenting what was a moot point.

Amara was on the way to my base, and she had to be stopped. But how?

Quickly, I rode Smoke through the dense throng of units cramming the platform area. My mind was no longer on the battles raging nearby, just the fluttering red banner at my base.

"Out of the way!" I shouted with frustration. Since I was the idiot who jammed them all together, I was now the idiot who had to get past them.

"Commander coming through!" soldiers shouted as they jostled each other to make room.

I navigated my way through the units until I emerged past the densest part of the formation. With a kick at Smoke, I headed down the southwest curve.

*Enemy spotted!*

It was one of the Lookouts at the Keep. Amara's icon appeared above the trees due north of their position.

Analyzing my map, I was alarmed to see that all buildings had each just started training units. Previous units had already moved on and were halfway to the middle. All of those were slow moving footmen save for one cavalry unit.

Grumbling curses, I selected the cavalry unit and ordered it back to base at top speed.

The only other defenders present at the base were the lookouts as well as one archer and one footmen unit. The latter two having been assigned to guard the banner.

For some reason I didn't think this would give Amara much cause for concern. If she felt she didn't have a chance to get the banner, this attack wouldn't be attempted.

I passed footmen units as I raced southward, and each one cheered in kind. I didn't feel celebratory. This had taken me completely by surprise, something Amara was good at. I needed to be the one full of surprises, for a change.

Halfway there, I got the footmen's leader onto a chat screen.

"You see her coming?" I asked, rhetorically. Of course he did. They all did. I just needed to hear him say so.

"Yes, Commander!" the footmen leader said. "And we are ready for her!"

I wished that were true.

"Let me see what she's doing," I said. By now, Amara's icon was slowing down as it sidled up next to the Keep.

The leader turned around giving me a view of the base.

The great eagle was hovering high above, with Amara peering downward, assessing the situation.

The Lookouts atop the Keep fired their crossbows, but their bolts came up short. I noticed with dread that reloading these weapons took the Lookouts forever.

My archer unit stood nearby, bows at the ready. They didn't even attempt to fire since Amara was well out of their range.

The footmen were assembled around the altar, eyes on the aerial invader.

What was she going to do?

I was still too far. Less than two minutes out.

The eagle adjusted its height and came in closer to the top of the Keep. The Lookouts were still loading their crossbows as quick as they could.

It wouldn't be fast enough.

The eagle reared its head back then opened its massive beak. Thrusting forward it let out a terrifying shriek.

It was using an ability.

The shriek emanating from the eagle was like a physical attack. The air in front of it shimmered like a heatwave. The Lookouts were enveloped in a torrent of deafening sound.

The Lookouts were knocked back and sent flying over the battlements. They tumbled screaming down the vast height of the Keep to the ground.

With this problem eliminated, Amara brought the eagle around the Keep and landed.

The archers moved close and loosened their bows.

But as the arrows zinged toward their mark, the eagle stood tall and flapped its mighty wings creating an incredible wind.

The arrows were knocked out of mid-flight as the wind intensified. In seconds, the eagle generated hurricane-force winds.

The archers tried to stand against this, but were sent flying to the ground, or tumbling into the trees.

While the great eagle maintained the attack with its wings, Amara jumped off its back.

The moment before she touched the ground she vanished.

Shadow Form.

My footmen, shocked by the attack on the archers, but still rooted to the spot I commanded them not to leave, looked about in confusion.

Oh, for the love of...

"Watch out!" I shouted at the footmen leader. "She's in Shadow Form!"

I rounded the final bend, and the Keep was in sight, but I was a good thirty seconds away.

The footmen looked about, apprehensive. They knew an enemy was nearby, but had no idea where.

Yuinnick continued its attack, buffeting the archers with the horrific wind. When one archer managed to get purchase and stand, he was immediately sent sprawling to the ground.

*Your Banner Has Been Taken!*

No, no, no, I thought. This cannot be happening. Not again!

Amara had snuck by the footmen in Shadow Form, but the moment she grabbed the banner she became visible. Crouched on the altar itself, banner grasped tightly in one hand, she killed the nearest surprised footman with a sword swing.

The other eleven footmen reacted, whirling to confront her.

The great eagle immediately stopped flapping its wings and charged forward at the footmen formation, shrieking loudly.

As some footmen engaged Amara, others turned to face the frightening champion moving in to attack.

I was ten seconds away.

Amara's sword was a blur of motion parrying sword swings from her perch on the skeletal altar. Surrounded and outnumbered, she appeared in a desperate fight to keep them at bay.

This attempt at the banner had been a tremendous risk to take. But fortune favors the bold, especially on the Battle Field.

Yuinnick snapped at a footman with its beak, slicing him in two. Then it crushed another with its massive talons while flapping its wings to keep balance. The great eagle moved in closer, forcing the footmen to scramble out of the way.

Amara noticed me galloping toward her and grinned while slicing the head off a footman.

"I'm coming for you!" I found myself shouting. My heart raced as the distance between us shrank.

Then Amara moved. She dodged a footman's sword swing, then rolled under another's attack.

Yuinnick brushed three footmen away with a giant wing, as if they were toys, and squatted down.

"No!" I yelled, changing my direction toward the great eagle.

Amara jumped and stepping off a fallen footman's back, leapt up and into Yuinnick's saddle.

The huge bird flapped its wings and launched up from the ground.

Unperturbed, I took Smoke directly under the eagle, its massive form blocking out the sky. Wings beat around me and the wind threatened to knock me to the grass.

But as Yuinnick ascended, I still had a chance at one desperate attempt to stop them.

I shifted from my saddle to my feet, and using my Leap ability, jumped straight up from Smoke's back.

The next second, I found myself clinging to a leathery leg of the eagle as it ascended northward into the sky.

Below, I saw Smoke running about in confusion. The remaining footman looked up at me in amazement.

For a few moments I could only marvel at my own folly. What had been the point of this?

It didn't appear that Yuinnick noticed my presence, so large was the creature.

We sped northward, and the dense forest below moved past at an alarming speed. Did Amara intend to go to the center altar?

A quick look showed that my forces still firmly controlled the platform and the area immediately north of it. But her own army was pressing forward. They were closer than before.

Not waiting to give her any more satisfaction at snatching my banner, again, I decided to try something really stupid. There were few options for me, anyway.

My legs and arms were wrapped around the thick leg of the eagle. I released my grip with one hand and summoned my sword. Then I stabbed upwards.

Yuinnick shrieked with pain and its flapping wings lurched in surprise.

As if in answer to my attack, the eagle started to descend. I stabbed again and blood flowed from the wound under its huge feathers.

Now Yuinnick tried to use the talons on its other leg to swipe at me, but it couldn't reach.

When I stabbed again, I felt us falling faster.

I looked down just in time to see us fly into the tops of the trees.

The branches smashed into me at horrific speed. I tried to hide behind the eagle's thick leg but it appeared to be willing to take more damage if it meant I would be knocked off.

It worked.

I couldn't hold on while being attacked by speeding trees, and I was smacked hard again, losing my grip.

I had one last glance of the eagle's mammoth form flapping away, a gold beam of light shooting upwards from its back where my banner was being carried away.

Crypt, here I come, I thought morbidly.

Then I plummeted through the forest canopy.

# CHAPTER FOURTEEN

My avatar bounced unceremoniously from branch to branch as I fell through the trees.

Reaching bottom, I did a hard face plant into the ground, and my screen went black.

Well, that didn't work, I thought. Various alternate scenarios played through my mind as I waited to be reborn, but none would have ended well. Perhaps I should have waited until we were closer to the platform before attacking the eagle? My archers could have lent some support.

Mentally, I shrugged. Didn't matter now. Amara had the banner, again. While I...

I looked curiously at my view-screen. Nothing had changed, the blackness remained. Then I noticed the icons still on the edge of my vision. They usually vanished while I was being reborn.

My health indicator was at 2%. Oh, crap. I wasn't dead!

Pushing forward, my avatar lifted her face out of the thick loam of the forest floor. I blinked in confusion at my surroundings. Trees, lots of them, crowded around me like towering guards.

Looking upwards I could see the blue sky high above. The path of my fall was clear from all the snapped branches.

Feeling like an idiot, I stood and brushed myself off.

Then I looked to the map.

Amara appeared within view of my fighting units at the middle. She circled the platform once, but my army were still firmly in control of it. If she landed, she would be swarmed.

Then, as if deciding now was not the time, she flew northward, and her icon eventually vanished as she passed out of view.

My army still fought a protracted war. Units crashed against enemy units. Formations on both sides morphed as the battle situation changed. Amara's army was gaining some ground, but my double block of units kept them back.

Still, it was only a matter of time. Now that she had my banner, she could sit back at her base and funnel a constant stream of trolls south. Eventually, she'd break through or simply wear me down. Then the platform would be hers.

And the game would be over.

Getting angry again, I started to make my way west, the shortest distance out of the forest according to the map.

This terrain was not meant for travel, at all. Most of the way I had to climb up from the cramped forest floor with its huge root system that intertwined to make a living barrier. Carefully, I leapt from branch to branch.

I was mindful of my health. Yeah, I could purposely take a tumble and be back in my base in thirty seconds. But Amara would get Battle Points for it. Even if she didn't directly kill me, her big bird was the one that dropped me. She'd get 100 points, and I wouldn't let her have them.

Before I emerged at the forest's edge I had called on Smoke, who ran up from the base to meet me. When I finally escaped the forest gymnasium he was there, nickering in welcome.

I climbed up into his saddle. "Let's get to the Keep."

As we headed south, I looked over the perpetual fight in the middle.

My units were smashed up against Amara's units and although she had more cavalry than I, more of my own horsemen were heading north or lined up down both approaches.

Grax still sat back from the main action, guarding the altar. His health had actually increased a little, perhaps to an innate regeneration ability for champions. But he still was not strong enough to move closer and assist. A single volley from an archer unit would do him in.

I was genuinely at a loss as to what do to next. Fight until Amara gained the platform through attrition?

As we arrived at my base, both the defending archer unit and footmen unit had retaken their positions. All their faces were sullen. In their minds, they had failed and lost the banner.

The cavalry unit I had redirected to the base stood by. I simply sent them north again.

"You fought well," I said to the defending units as I dismounted. "And against difficult odds."

This only seemed to mollify them slightly.

What else could be said? The banner was gone.

Before entering the Keep I looked northward. Far in the distance were two thread-thin beams of light.

Wonderful.

I also noted my scout had been spotted and killed by archers. Great.

I entered the Keep and sat in the middle of the floor. Above, a Lookout waved at me from the trapdoor and returned to duty.

At least the Lookouts respawn on their own, I thought absentmindedly.

As I watched my health regenerate, I glared at the unit icons on the map. This was not fun. Losing, that is. Worse, the knowledge I was going to lose, regardless, sucked even more.

Amara was in possession of both banners.

I could attempt to fight my way to her base. Even if successful, it could take forever to get there. I'd also have to secure both approaches because while concentrating on one, the other could be a threat to my advancing army's flank.

I looked at the map with its figure-eight formation and the grass plains which funneled units around like circles of death.

The trees were more than just a resource they were an impediment, too. So thickly packed that even a footmen unit could not pass through them.

Suddenly, I was struck with a thought.

I scrutinized the map more closely. Could it work?

Only one way to find out.

With my health bar at 100%, I left the Keep. Outside, I mounted Smoke. To the footmen and archer unit leaders, I said, "Hold fast while I'm gone."

They snapped a salute. "Yes, Commander!"

Part of me blamed them for letting the banner be taken, but really the blame was all mine. Inexperienced and completely unprepared, I'd let Amara have the upper hand this entire time.

I rode northwest at a hard gallop. By the midway point of the bend I passed units who were waiting in line to get to middle and more were still coming from the base. Crazy.

One giant grindfest.

Maybe I could change that.

As I approached the final northern bend toward the middle, I kept Smoke close to the outer tree line. It was possible an enemy scout was watching me, but I decided to minimize the risk of being seen.

Roughly fifty paces before the turn opened up to the middle clearing, I jumped to the ground and dismissed Smoke.

Several of my units were in line here and everyone gave a wave and a cheer.

I grimaced. So much for keeping a low profile.

Then I slipped into Shadow Form.

Keeping to just within the trees I continued around the bend and headed east.

The mass of units got more dense as everyone crowded toward the platform, the only river crossing.

As I approached the last few trees before the clearing I could hear the ferocious fighting taking place just ahead. Screams of men dying, horses in pain, arrows zinging about, sword and spears clashing.

But there was another sound, just a short distance past the tree line.

Rushing water.

Carefully, I entered the forest at the western edge of the middle – the pinched waist of the map's figure eight.

I climbed over bulging roots and ducked under thick branches. Then the trees opened up to the river which flowed from somewhere deeper in the forest to the west and continued on to the middle platform to the east, just beyond my view.

The river was a good twenty paces across here and looked deep. No one was meant to cross it, such was its design.

No army units, anyway.

Using as much available ground as I could, I ran at the water. At the river's edge, I jumped. I used my Leap ability, which I'd been diligently assigning skill points to over the last few character levels.

These points paid off.

I landed on a massive root on the opposite bank.

Fearing an ambush of some kind, I froze in place, sword at the ready.

The only thing that assaulted me was the sound of the raging river and the cacophony of battle through the trees to the east.

After the count of ten, I moved, quickly and quietly. There was still the possibility of a scout nearby, so stealth was crucial.

Trying to ignore my fighting troops so close by, I headed due north. Something more important needed my immediate attention other than commanding doomed units.

I was going to take Amara's banner.

# CHAPTER FIFTEEN

I cautiously made my way north, navigating the barrier of trees. It was slow going considering the forest was not meant to be traversed, but it made me relatively confident I would not be detected.

To the east I sometimes caught glimpses of troll units. Enemy units were so bunched up in the middle that they, too, had to line up and wait for their turn.

I kept my focus on the difficult terrain ahead. Jumping from branch to branch, scaling tree trunks, and avoiding impassible clusters of roots took all my concentration.

Soon, I was nearing the final northern turn to Amara's base, according to my map. The trees were even closer together here, and I decided to leave the forest and follow the tree line the rest of the way. As long as I was careful, I would be able to get close.

I changed direction to the east and dropped from a branch.

And landed right next to a troll scout.

I froze in surprise.

The troll scout whirled around, eyes wide with apprehension.

He did not look directly at me, but cast his gaze about trying to find the source of the sound.

Even this close, my Shadow Form was good, being completely maxed out at 10/10 ability points. The forest was nothing but dark shadows and, as a result, made me fully invisible.

With a dagger in his hand, the scout slowly turned to take in his surroundings. I was only two paces from where he crouched.

Eliminating him would be easy, but then Amara would see the scout's death message and know instantly where I was.

I kept perfectly still and watched nervously as the scout continued to scan the area.

Suddenly, the scout took a step forward, dagger in front of him.

Uh-oh.

The green humanoid's large black eyes darted this way and that.

Great, I had to spook a real nervous one.

He took another step forward and the tip of his dagger nearly touched my vest.

Shadow Form would be lost the moment I engaged in combat, like striking out at the scout, or with physical contact.

Holding my breath I leaned back. I wanted to try to move away but I could not be certain of my footing where I landed.

This close I could see the incredible detail of the troll's features. The pores in his green oily skin, the bristly hair that jutted out of his huge nostrils like pitchforks.

This game was so realistic that even his breath stank like a fetid wind wafting over a slop pile.

For several long agonizing moments the scout stood like this. Eyes scanning, dagger inches from my chest.

Then, the scout relaxed and snorted. He turned away and moved southward, slinking through the trees. Soon, he vanished from view.

I sighed with relief and resumed my own way.

At the tree line, I paused. The plains curved due west from here and continued south to the middle.

A cavalry unit rumbled by, shaking the ground. None of the troll riders glanced in my direction.

Keeping close to the trees I went west until the forest ended at a large clearing.

Amara's base.

It did not look that much different than mine, only she had three of each unit's buildings for quicker training. These were lined up side by side next to her Keep.

The Keep had been upgraded, too. Troll Lookouts with crossbows watched from the tower's crown.

From the top of the keep emanated the golden beam of light indicating the location of a banner. My banner.

Amara was inside with it. But what for? Added protection? Made sense. She could not be assassinated while safely hidden away within the walls of the Keep.

Admittedly, I had hoped to catch Amara unaware and back-stab her causing her to drop my banner. But that pleasure appeared to be denied from me. For now.

This was another tactic I took note of for future use. If you have the banner but can't win, hide.

I scanned the rest of the base and was surprised to see she had a gold mine right next to her Keep. She didn't have to go looking for her gold like I did. Instead, she lucked out and had the gold right at her starting area. I could see workers digging furiously away and bringing buckets of gold out of the mine and dumping the nuggets into a huge iron hopper.

A little further north at the tree line was a quarry. So she had that near her starting point, too.

This explained how she was able to attack me so early in the game. Everything was here to help her get started with minimal delay.

Plant the banner, build the keep, get the first worker unit, build the barracks, train the grunts and rush south.

I tried not to feel annoyed, but failed.

Directly north of the Keep was the skeletal altar. A blue banner fluttered in the wind within the grasp of a skeletal hand.

Slumped next to the altar, large and terrifying, was Yuinnick. The great eagle didn't look to be in good health and its eyes were closed as if sleeping. In fact, its health indicator was less than 10%. I must have inflicted a bleeding wound on the champion causing it to lose so much health.

It was probably slowly regenerating like Grax.

Looking about I noticed no units assigned to guarding the altar, let alone the base.

Everything Amara had was at the middle or on its way there.

As I surveyed Amara's domain, an army unit emerged from each of the buildings having finished their training. They immediately marched or galloped off, some via the southwest passage, the rest the southeast.

Perfect. All the buildings were starting to train again, which meant I had about five minutes.

With a final look around I detached from the tree line and moved toward the altar. As I approached, my eyes danced from Yuinnick, to the Lookouts above, and to the Keep door which was closed.

When I arrived at the altar, I paused. Yuinnick was the closest threat but was oblivious to my presence. It seemed lost in its regeneration process.

The blue banner fluttered in the wind.

The moment I grabbed this, all hell was going to break loose.

Okay, Vee, you can do this, I thought.

I took a deep breath and reached for the banner's wooden handle.

The Keep's door suddenly slammed open.

I froze, hand an inch from the banner.

Amara bolted out of the door and marched in my direction looking angry. In one hand was my banner.

Uh-oh.

Maintaining my Shadow Form, I summoned my sword and tensed for a fight.

But instead of coming at me she went to Yuinnick, who's eyes blinked open at her approach.

"This is taking too long," Amara said. I couldn't tell if that was directed at the eagle or she was just talking to herself.

She jumped up into the great eagle's saddle.

She's leaving! I thought with jubilation. This would make snatching her banner that much easier.

As Amara settled in, Yuinnick flapped his wings in preparation for take off.

The strong winds it produced caused the banner next to me to flutter wildly.

As the long blue banner whipped in the wind, the end of it curled around to graze my outstretched hand.

At its touch, my Shadow Form shimmered slightly for a moment, like a heat wave in a desert.

Amara happened to be looking in my general direction, and suddenly her head snapped over to look directly at me.

Uh-oh.

The elven woman's eyes widened with alarm. "You!" she screamed.

Time to go!

Without wasting another moment I grabbed the banner and my Shadow Form dropped.

*You Have the Enemy Banner!*

The next instant I summoned Smoke who appeared beside me.

"You FILTERED!" Amara roared. She screamed at the Lookouts to shoot at me.

As I leapt onto Smoke, a crossbow bolt actually ricocheted off the banner's wooden pole with a loud twang.

I kicked at Smoke's sides and we were off.

Behind me, Amara was shouting filtered obscenities at me, then at Yuinnick for not moving fast enough. But within moments, she had the great eagle champion lifting off in pursuit.

This is nuts, I thought. What I was doing was crazy.

Instead of following the plains in either direction that lead to the middle, I headed straight for the wall of forest directly south.

From somewhere above and behind me I heard the flapping of giant wings. A bolt zinged past my head.

Go! Go! Go!

The trees got closer.

A huge shadow fell over me and I turned to see Yuinnick's giant talons reaching down for me.

With a shout of surprise I jumped off of Smoke. At that moment, the mammoth bird snatched the horse and lifted him off the ground.

As I tumbled to the earth, I barely managed to keep a hold of the banner. Quickly, I ran straight at the trees as fast as my legs would carry me.

Behind me I heard Amara shouting at the eagle and heard Smoke drop heavily to the ground and whinny in pain.

*You Mount has been killed.*

Sorry, buddy, I thought grimly, running like a Shadow possessed.

The trees got closer.

Wind buffeted me from behind, again, and the eagle's shadow fell over me.

From my peripheral vision I saw the tip of a great black talon start to curl around me.

Letting out a shout I charged into the forest.

Yuinnick's outstretched feet practically propelled me forward, and I dived between two huge oaks.

I heard the eagle crash into the trees, and it shrieked. Branches snapped and wings flapped with the impact.

But instead of looking back I kept going. Tumbling, jumping and ducking under branches.

Soon, the sounds of the great eagle and the filtered shouts of Amara were diffused by the thick foliage.

Heart pounding, and lungs bursting, I moved as quickly as the terrain would allow.

As I moved southward, I realized I was grinning like a maniac and even laughed.

I had Amara's banner!

Next stop: The platform altar.

# CHAPTER SIXTEEN

I ran as fast as I could manage, but the very terrain conspired to slow me to a crawl.

My heart still pounded hard in my chest and I felt gallons of sweat pour over my body under the simulation suit. I was elated to the point of being giddy looking at the magnificent blue banner in my possession.

But I didn't fool myself into thinking I had won in any way. Not even close. In fact, the hard part was just beginning.

The crush of units at the middle intensified, no doubt because Amara was now increasing the pressure to seize the platform.

My units were fighting heroically, but even now I could see they were being pushed back. Both prongs of formations had shifted southward and now formed a single front.

Above the forest canopy, I heard Yuinnick screech and flap its mighty wings. Amara was in pursuit. And even though I couldn't see her, her icon was prominent on the map right above mine.

Would she drop down and attack me? It would mean giving up the support of her eagle champion as the huge bird could never get through even the top portion of the forest canopy.

As I progressed southward, Amara circled above. She was trying to think of what to do. Good. Let her fret for once.

After following me well past the halfway point of the circular forest, Amara flew southward to the middle area.

I allowed myself the slightest feeling of relief. Fighting her in this terrain would not have been ideal, and I suspected she knew the odds of winning would weigh heavily in favor with who owned the platform. So that was where she would go.

It was also my only destination.

I considered hiding out in the forest indefinitely. Amara would eventually have to come in and confront me. But that would be pointless and extend this Battle Field nonsense for ages.

No, I wanted this stupid game to be over and done with, once and for all. And I would do it by not hiding or avoiding a fight, like Amara did back at her Keep.

This would be settled where it was intended to take place all along.

The middle platform.

Soon I was within about fifty paces of the southern edge of the forest. Even at this distance and with all the trees enclosed around me, I could hear the intense sounds of combat.

On my map could be seen all the unit icons jammed so close they practically overlapped each other.

I zoomed in for a clearer picture of what was happening and immediately spotted a problem.

The forest edge was lined with enemy units which only minutes before was under my units' control.

They were blocking my way to the platform.

I scoffed. This had to be Amara's doing. She knew I would emerge from the forest at that location and did everything she could to get her men into position there. In fact, I now noticed the entire forest was encircled by enemy units. Amara had me completely surrounded.

Quickly, I gave commands to my troops defending the northern edge of the platform to push north toward the trees. Each unit leader confirmed the order, but looking at the crush of enemies they were facing, I doubted it would do much good.

Still, I had to try. Sitting and waiting for something to occur was not in my DNA, much to my detriment.

Skulking forward, I drew closer to the forest edge. Movement could be seen between the trees as men and horses fought in the middle clearing.

Then I saw them. Grunts fumbling through the trees in my direction. Dozens of them. Watching them try to negotiate the tangle of foliage was laughable. But they were slowly making progress.

They were coming for me.

Not wanting to retreat, I climbed. I had grown slightly adapt at scaling the trees here as I'd gotten so much recent practice. In the upper canopy, I jumped from branch to branch, and from tree to tree, making my way southward.

Below I heard shouting and caught the occasional glance of a grunt staring up at me. If they wanted to come up here, let them try.

One grunt threw his spear, and it thunked into the bark next to my feet. Others started in kind and soon spears where swishing through the surrounding air, some striking close by.

I moved faster, mindful of my balance.

Then I reached the very edge of the forest and from the safety of a huge branch thick with leaves, peered downward at the chaos below.

Amara's units had now pushed right up against the northern edge of the platform. My units were fighting like rabid animals to keep them back but the pressure was too great.

Past the platform were the mass assembly of my own army waiting to join in.

Arrows flew from every direction. Screams and death were everywhere. The carnage was staggering.

Sensing something amiss, I turned and looked behind me.

Amazingly, two grunts had managed to climb the tree and were now trying to take aim at me with their spears.

Time to go.

With a final glance at the mass of enemy units between me and the platform, I jumped outward through the leaves. My Leap ability kicked in and I found myself soaring through the air.

A swarm of arrows zipped by me in the same direction, fired only a moment before my jump. Several struck me along my right side and in an instant my health bar dropped by half.

As I fell downward amongst the arrow cloud, I had the strange arrow-eye view of their trajectory.

But I came up short of the platform.

Instead, I landed right on the shoulders of a troll cavalry leader who grunted with the impact. Someone managed to slice my left thigh with a sword and nearly caused me to fall.

Even injured, I could still use my momentum and jumped from the cavalry leader and sailed over the front lines.

An attempt at a graceful landing was foiled by my odd angle and extensive injuries, and I tumbled across the platform to slam hard against the altar.

For a few seconds, my avatar could only see stars.

Arrows landed around me, and someone was screaming at me to get back. I looked up to see a footman leader trying to help me but an arrow punctured his temple and he fell from my wobbly view.

Well, I'm here, I thought, trying to stand.

Human cavalry and footmen created a line across the platform only a few paces from the altar. A massive crush of enemy units pressed against them.

I'm losing the platform.

Grax loomed over me. "You are injured." He said, log-club on his shoulder.

His health bar was worse than mine. "You, too," I said.

Suddenly, the sky darkened.

It was Amara on Yuinnick circling overhead. She was low to the ground, and I ordered all my archers to change their targets to her.

As arrows shot up toward her, she dived.

"Death now," Grax said, hefting his weapon. "It shall be glorious."

I blinked at the red banner in my hand. What was I just standing here for?

Quickly, I whirled about and jammed the banner's handle into the waiting skeletal hand.

*Blue Banner has been captured! Five minute countdown begins!*

A counter appeared on my view-screen, but I didn't have time to even notice.

Amara practically fell from the sky and slammed into me. We tumbled across the crowded platform, bouncing against the legs of horses and men.

As I skidded to a halt, I saw Yuinnick fly straight into Grax who dropped his club at the last moment to grab the giant bird with both arms.

With a loud thump both champions shot across the platform and vanished over the edge. A huge splash of water geysered upwards when they hit the river.

Amara had recovered and stood with sword in one hand, and my red banner in the other.

"Time to fail, you miserable FILTERED!" she yelled.

Before I could retort a footman stepped out of the front line crush and stabbed her right through her abdomen, its point sticking out her back.

Screaming in pain Amara dropped my banner where it landed in an upright position right at the edge of the platform above the river.

*Your Banner Has Been Dropped!*

Amara's health bar dropped to less than 20% and she grabbed her injured side with her free hand. With her sword she decapitated the footman.

Stunned, I moved toward my banner. If I could just nudge it off the platform, it would be returned. Or maybe since it hadn't been placed in the altar it would be instantly returned at my touch. One way to find out.

But as I moved, Amara staggered forward and swung her sword at me.

Losing blood fast, I only just managed to parry it away.

"This isn't over, FILTERED," she yelled over the fighting around us and coughed up blood. "I still have time."

"You're getting your butt spanked by a noob," I said with a bloody grin. "I'll post it on all the forums. I promise you."

This got her really angry, and she lunged forward.

But as we swung at each other with weakening blows, a shadow fell over us.

Looking up I saw two sets of massive arrow clouds falling toward us. Dozens from her side, dozens from mine.

Then they found their mark. Arrows hit me over several places across my body.

I heard Amara scream in pain.

As I fell over and my vision dimmed to nothing, two messages appeared before me.

*You have been slain in battle!*

*Amara Frostwalker has been slain in battle!*

Then my screen went black.

# CHAPTER SEVENTEEN

It was all I could do but stare at the two death messages in amazement.

We both died? What now? What about the banners?

Amara's banner was still in the grip of the skeletal altar, while mine sat perched on the platform's edge. And now no one was there to return either.

Thankfully, neither could any of our units. Only players could carry or return a banner.

I thought of what filtered obscenities Amara must be screaming at her screen right now and laughed. If it was any consolation, we were both on the same respawn timer and the same distance from the middle.

Whoever got there first would have the advantage.

*Four Minute Warning!*

I grinned at the timer message. Amara would have received it, too. I'm sure many more filtered words were being spit out by her at that moment. And there was nothing she could do about it, being dead and all.

Still, it underscored the need for me to get to the middle and fast.

After thirty seconds had counted down, I appeared in the crypt – again. This was becoming a bad habit. I jumped off the slab and raced up the narrow stone steps.

Once in the Keep, I ran out the door only offering the Lookout above an over-the-shoulder wave.

I summoned Smoke, and we took off to the western curve. Units of various types were lined up even down here, so long was the back up to fight at the middle. Many waved and cheered me on perhaps sensing something major was about to happen.

I sensed it, too. But considering how Amara had surprised me so much, I feared for an ignominious loss.

As we raced past the western curve and drove northward another message appeared.

*Three Minute Warning!*

My eyes locked on the map. Unit icons were on unit icons and through all that mess it looked as if possession of the platform was evenly split, for now.

Based on past runs north, I figured I'd get to the platform in a little over two minutes. But as for Amara?

Realizing something, I quickly scrolled through my combat log while Smoke charged northward.

The combat log was long. Like, really long. It detailed every attack by nearby units and then listed deaths and victories when I wasn't in the vicinity.

I quickly scrolled back to just after I died. There I saw two messages.

*Yuinnick, the Champion, has died in battle.*

That meant Amara could no longer fly. Thank the Gaming Gods. Now she'd have to muck about on the ground with the rest of us mortals.

But there was another message directly below it.

*Grax, the Champion, has died in battle.*

That genuinely saddened me, but I was not surprised. His health was nearly gone, and he wanted to die while fighting. He got his wish and in doing so removed a vital threat from Amara's arsenal.

As I approached the final bend toward the middle, I spotted Amara's icon on the map heading southward from the eastern curve.

Dang, she was fast. Too fast.

I kicked at Smoke's sides, but it didn't increase the poor mount's speed.

*Two Minute Warning!*

We rounded the bend to the middle clearing. The platform was so jammed with units, both on it and around, I couldn't see the altar anymore. Just the twin golden beams of light projecting upwards from the banners.

Then I spotted Amara. She was trying to negotiate her white mare through the throng of trolls. Even from this distance I could tell she was yelling and screaming at everyone in her way.

I had a similar problem and kept to the furthest edge of the approach along the northern tree line, the same one I'd crossed into before heading to Amara's base. Still, units were crowding up against the trees.

"Make way! Commander coming through!" I yelled over the din. The message was relayed along and units did their best to let me pass, but the crush of bodies and horses was incredible.

A glance told me that Amara and I were roughly the same distance from the platform.

I kicked and swore and pushed my way through the crowd. But just a dozen paces away from the platform's southern edge Smoke could not move any further.

I contemplated dismounting but that would make my progress even worse, even impossible.

Then a gray figure caught my eye.

From the opposite side of the platform, Amara had jumped. She sailed over the crushing throng and vanished into the crowd on the platform itself.

*One Minute Warning!*

Fine, I thought. If it's good for her, it's good for me, too.

From Smoke's back I stood and angled myself at where I wanted to land.

*The Blue Banner Has Been Taken!*

No!

I jumped and with my Leap ability, sailing over the crush of men and horses beneath me.

Up above, I clearly saw the altar and Amara was standing on it holding the blue banner. She needed to get it off the platform but her attention was at her feet.

Amazingly a footman had grabbed onto her leg with both hands, preventing her from moving.

Cool! I thought as I fell upon her, sword swinging.

With bizarre luck she sensed me near her and she spun about to block my attack. I collided with her and we both fell over the altar and into the mad crush around it.

Even as we landed, we still swung at each other although she was hampered by carrying her banner in one hand.

"Going somewhere?" I yelled as we both scampered to our feet.

"FILTERED!" she screamed, facing off against me. "Go return your banner! It's over there!"

"I may be a noob, but I'm not stupid," I said. What did I care about my banner now? Going for it would guarantee she could get her own banner off the platform. Then this mess would start all over again.

A troll rider accidentally bumped his horse up against Amara. She spun around and slashed at him causing the mount to kick and split the skull of a troll grunt.

I lunged forward and stabbed her in the shoulder. But as I did so, an arrow hit me in the stomach and pierced deeply, all the way to its fletching.

Uh-oh.

*Thirty Second Warning!*

My health dropped to less than half within an instant.

Amara, for her part, didn't care. Instead, she was trying to push her way through the crowd. I realized she wanted to get to the edge of the platform over the water. Once there, her banner would be returned.

Despite my near fatal wound, I swung at her again and again. Each time she would parry while pushing her way slowly backwards through the crowd.

The noise was deafening with screams of the dying and the constant clashing of steel.

*Twenty Second Warning!*

So obsessed with getting the banner to the edge, Amara tried to pull away from me all together. She was scared. Not of me, but of losing.

As I attempted to step closer a troll grunt stumbled over to block me. Angered, I slashed at him, but he managed to parry the blow. Behind him Amara turned around and faced the direction of the river. She was going to try to throw the banner over!

I dodged the troll's lunge and slashed the tip of the spear off followed by his head, for good measure.

*Ten Second Warning!*

Amara suddenly threw the banner. But a cluster of cavalry riders, both human and troll, were directly in her way, fighting. The banner rose up but smacked against the side of a human rider and fell to the ground, standing up.

*The Blue Banner Has Been Dropped!*

I swung at Amara, and this time because her attention was on her banner, she was slow to block it. A bloody gash appeared across her right shoulder.

She was shouting, but I couldn't really hear her. It sounded like no, no, no, over and over again.

With a sword feint in my direction that I foolishly backed away from, she lunged at the banner and grabbed it again.

*The Blue Banner Has Been Taken!*

I suddenly found myself pushed from behind by a horse's flank and I crashed into Amara who yelped in surprise.

*Five Second Warning!*

But the horse didn't just push me, it fell over with a horrible cry and landed right on me and Amara.

*The Blue Banner Has Been Dropped!*

*Four Seconds!*

Amara and I were pinned from the waist down under the horse.

We were right near the edge of the platform. The blue banner stood upright on the very edge, almost teetering over.

Desperately, she stretched outward toward the banner with a painful scream, while locking swords with me via her other hand.

*Three Seconds!*

I grabbed at her outstretched arm, but the movement only served to help her touch the banner's wooden pole with the tip of her fingers.

With my sword arm I kept it pushed up against her own.

*Two Seconds!*

Amara ignored me completely and stretched all she could. The tips of her fingers nudged the banner. The banner moved several millimeters and began to teeter.

Frustrated, I quickly switched the sword with my bow, which remained pressed up against her weapon.

*One Second!*

I summoned my magma arrow. As it appeared in my quiver, I instantly reached back to snatch it then nocked and fired the molten projectile directly into Amara's face at point blank range.

Then the deafening sound around me suddenly stopped.

Everything froze, like pausing a movie. I blinked in surprise. The magma arrow, sticking out of Amara's eye, had just begun to boil its way through her skull.

I took a screenshot.

Then she vanished. The horse that held me down vanished. The soldiers and trolls around me vanished. And so did the rest of the world until all that remained was a white void.

Then a message appeared, the words hanging in the empty space before me.

*Vivian Valesh is Victorious!*

# CHAPTER EIGHTEEN

For several long moments, I stared at the floating message.

My heart still pounded in my chest, my breath heavy and near gasping.

I won.

The realization didn't click in right away, but the Battle Field was gone and the fighting was over.

I won!

Astonished, I pushed myself up from the nonexistent ground to stand.

I defeated Amara. Better yet, I defeated Amara in my very first Battle Field gaming session.

Somewhere out past the white void, in the real world, the player who controlled Amara was cursing up the mother of all filtered storms.

I laughed until tears rolled down my face and collected at the bottom of my view-screen.

Beautiful.

The void dissolved into a swirl of colors and I found myself standing back in the cavern chamber on its middle rise, where this mess had all started.

As I looked around, I shouted in surprise and summoned my sword.

All the skeletons in the chamber who had been laying on the ground, now stood facing me. Each one pointed at me with an outstretched arm.

What was this? Another final fight?

Rumbling laughter made me turn about.

Y'Godda's spirit stood beside me, resplendent in his bright white armor.

"Don't worry, adventurer. They will not harm you. They only wish to congratulate you on your victory over such a skilled opponent."

"Yeah, okay," I said trying not to sound doubtful. Funny way to congratulate someone. But if they weren't going to attack, I'd take it.

"And, I too, wish to offer my congratulations," Y'Godda said, grinning from ear to ear.

"Thanks," I said. "It was tough, but a fun learning experience."

Learning experience was an understatement. Trial by fire would be a better analogy.

Y'godda nodded, his long red beard rasping against his armor. "Yes, I know this was your very first Battle Field. You performed well. Especially considering the experience of your opponent."

"Oh?" I said, curious. "How experienced is she?"

"According to the records, Amara Frostwalker has never been defeated in over 118 Battle Field conflicts. This would be her first."

I burst out laughing, again. Oh, fantastic! I wish I could see Amara's face right now.

"Speaking of my opponent," I said looking around the chamber. "Where did she go?"

Y'godda frowned. "Unfortunately, your opponent left the world before the final message of her loss could be given to her."

"Left the world?"

"I believe you mortals refer to her action as 'Rage-Quit.'"

My laughter echoed off the cavern walls for several long moments. Knowing Amara rage-quit was even better than seeing her face after the fact.

Eventually, I picked myself up off the ground and gave Y'godda my full attention again.

"Sorry," I said. "Couldn't help myself."

"Hmm," said the dead general. "So, Vivian Valesh, it is time for your reward. The one you fought ever so valiantly for." He waved a hand.

Upon the rise a banner appeared. It was neither red nor blue, but a brilliant white.

"Cool," I said. Looking at the Lost War Banner of Y'Godda made me feel a little weak-kneed. Before, it had been a simple item to obtain after a long quest-chain. Now, it was a symbol of my victory over my own self-doubts while trying to win it.

It also symbolized my defeat of Amara, which made it all the more special.

Reaching forward, I grasped the banner's wooden handle and lifted. It came free easily.

*Quest Update: Y'Godda Be Kidding Me.*

*You have found the Lost War Banner of Y'Godda after many trials. Return it to the quest giver for your final quest reward.*

"Nice," I said. Suddenly, the surrounding chamber changed, and I found myself standing in a clearing.

I was outside the cavern, its huge stone door now shut and sealed with a magical barrier again, ready for the next adventurer to come.

"Well, goodbye to you, too," I said with a shrug. Y'Godda must not have believed in adventurers lingering in his dank cavern for longer than necessary.

I summoned Smoke and jumped into his saddle. With the banner over one shoulder, we rode through the Forest of Dreams. There was one final destination to be reached.

After crossing through several travel-gates, I stepped into a blighted realm, full of black mountains and dead forests.

I followed a crooked path along the shores of a blood red lake which waters were still as glass. The path ended at the front gate of a ruined castle, its walls decimated and crumbling.

As I dismounted a chat request appeared at the lower part of my view-screen.

I looked at the caller's name in shock.

It was Amara.

I blinked in confusion. What could she possibly want to 'chat' with me about? How much she hated me? Or how much I didn't deserve to win?

The image of her angry, screaming face filled my mind's eye.

Any communication with her would be packed with filtered words. I decided to not give her the pleasure of swearing at me ever again.

Instead of accepting the chat, I dismissed it. Then I went into my chat settings and placed Amara Frostwalker on my Blocked Players list. Now she'd no longer have the ability to communicate with me in any way.

There, I thought. Defeated again.

With a laugh, I entered the ruined castle.

There, sitting upon an ancient throne, was a dark figure. My quest giver. Above his head was a name tile. Togish the Sullied.

"You have returned," said Togish as he watched me approach. "I am... surprised."

I stood before Togish and bowed my head slightly. "I did not want to disappoint you, oh great one."

Hey, I might not be the best role-player in the game, but it didn't stop me from trying.

Togish nodded. He was clad in burnt armor which had been melted to his blackened skin. According to lore Togish died in this very castle by dragon fire. Dragons sent by Y'Godda.

"I see you have the banner."

"Yes, great one."

He held out a blackened hand, with burnt flesh hanging from its fingers.

I presented the banner to Togish and the undead king snatched it from my hands.

*Quest Completed! Y'Godda Be Kidding Me*

*You have returned the Lost Banner of Y'Godda to Togish the Sullied.*

Togish grinned at the banner, his melted lips making the expression ghoulish. "Very good, adventurer. It has been a long time coming. With this, I am now one step closer to conquering the Realm of the Dead."

Uh-huh, I thought. Good luck with that, buddy. Just gimme my dang reward!

I kept my mouth shut and my head bowed.

Togish placed the banner onto a skeletal altar almost identical to the ones from the Battle Field. A bony hand grabbed the wooden handle.

Immediately, the banner's brightness faded and dulled to nothing. The magical wind that kept its banner flowing stopped as if whatever essence had been inside it died.

"And now for your reward," Togish said, drawing my attention away from the sad-looking banner.

He held out a burnt hand which gripped a quest scroll.

Bowing my head again in a gesture of thanks, I carefully took the scroll into my possession.

*Item received: Quest Scroll.*

*Reward: 14,000 Experience Points.*

Then another, flashier, message appeared.

*You have increased a level! You are now level 46! Congratulations!*

*Earned: 3 Attribute points, 5 Skill points, and 3 Ability points.*

Togish looked down at me. I tried not to stare at the hole in the middle of his face where his nose used to be. "You will find this particular quest... difficult. I know of no one who have survived its trials."

Neither had I, which made me all the more excited to finally have the chance to take a crack at it.

"I will endeavor to do my best, great one."

"If you do obtain its reward, see me again. We may have further business to do together."

I bowed one last time and backed away. Looking up I saw that Togish had turned from me, forgotten. He stared at the limp banner, nodding with satisfaction.

Hastily, I left the destroyed castle and got back on Smoke. Turning him to the path we made our way back to the travel gate.

I took this time to apply my new points.

2 Attribute points went right into Strength. This placed me within range of a host of high-level weaponry, particularly bows.

The third point I stuck in Agility. Can't have enough of that as a Shadow.

I put all five Skill points into Parry. Fending of spears and swords during the battle underscored the need for it to be shored up. A lot.

For my Ability Points, I placed 1 into Leap bringing it up to 4 out of 10.

Another went into Sure Shot, boosting it to 8 out of 10.

Now that I was level 46, a new Ability became available to me under my Offensive skill tree.

*Night Leech (0/8)*

*Level 46*

*Bladed Weapon Required*

*This attack allows the transfer of 15% of an opponent's hit points to the player. 10 minute cooldown. Next level grants a 20% transfer.*

Sweet. I assigned my last point into it and the Ability became available to me.

Would've been nice to use this on Amara. Maybe one day I'd get the chance.

Finished, I took one last look at my stats.

*Name: Vivian Valesh*

*Race: Human*

*Class: Thief*

*Subclass: Shadow*

*Level: 46, 0% toward next level*

*Hit Points: 1250, Mana: 120*
*Attributes:*
*Strength: 37*
*Agility: 46*
*Constitution: 40*
*Wisdom: 15*
*Intelligence: 15*
*Charisma: 20*
*Main Skills: (Level 3 or greater)*
*Archery: Level 8, 82%*
*Acrobatics: Level 3, 56%*
*Climbing: Level 7, 20%*
*Dodge: Level 7, 12%*
*Parry: Level 6, 58%*
*Sneak: Level 7, 42%*
*Swords: Level 9, 73%*
*Minor Skills: (Under level 3 - Select to view)*

Satisfied, I swiped the stats sheet away and returned to basking in the glory of returning the banner.

I was happy beyond words. In my hands I had the quest. Not any old quest, but *the* quest. Its final reward was the single most sought after item for players of my class.

And I was determined to be the very first to complete it.

As I moved along the path to take my leave of this dead realm, my mind was no longer on banners or Battle Fields or even Amara.

I became consumed with the quest contained in the scroll, which would lead me to the next item in my Shadow Master's Legendary armor set:

*The Shadow Blade.*

Vivian's adventure continues in
Shadow Blade

Shadow Blade
(Shadow For Hire Series)

**A hallowed weapon hidden in a jungle hell.**

Forced to prove my worthiness to an elite group of players, I must earn the right to enter one of the most notorious locations in the game.

The Emerald Caldera has a fearsome reputation for chewing up would-be adventurers and quickly sending them back to the newbie zone. Filled with dungeon temples, monstrous beasts and dark-magic cults, the jungles of this mysterious island are deserving of respect.

And I must plunge headlong into them because it is here where I can find the next elusive item in my Legendary Armor Set:

The Shadow Blade

AVAILABLE NOW

<u>Kingdom Level One</u>
<u>(Kingdom Series Book 1)</u>

**A broken kingdom for a reluctant king.**

Robert was content with his life as a night-shift janitor. No stress, no worries, and no responsibilities. But this idyllic existence is turned upside down when he suddenly finds himself trapped inside a fantasy Role Playing Game.

Confused and alone he must find a way to escape back to his own world and, more importantly, to his daughter. But to do that he must take up the biggest responsibility of all:

To rule a kingdom.

<u>AVAILABLE NOW</u>